MAGICAL STORIES

Look out for all of these enchanting story collections

by Enid Blyton

Animal Stories
Cherry Tree Farm
Christmas Stories
Christmas Tales
Christmas Treats
Christmas Wishes
Fireworks in Fairyland
Five-Minute Stories
Five-Minute Summer Stories
Goodnight Stories
Magical Fairy Tales
Mr Galliano's Circus
Nature Stories
Pet Stories
Rainy Day Stories
Spellbinding Stories
Springtime Stories
Stories for Bedtime
Stories for Christmas
Stories of Magic and Mischief
Stories of Mischief Makers
Stories of Rotten Rascals
Stories of Spells and Enchantments
Stories of Tails and Whiskers
Stories of Wizards and Witches
Stories of Wonders and Wishes
Summer Adventure Stories
Summertime Stories
Tales of Tricks and Treats
The Wizard's Umbrella
Winter Stories

Enid Blyton®

MAGICAL STORIES

Illustrations by Mark Beech

HODDER

HODDER CHILDREN'S BOOKS

This collection first published in Great Britain in 2024 by Hodder & Stoughton

1 3 5 7 9 10 8 6 4 2

A CIP catalogue record for this book is available from the British Library.

ISBN 978 1 444 97471 3

Typeset in Caslon Twelve by Palimpsest Book Production Ltd, Falkirk, Stirlingshire

Printed and bound in Great Britain by Clays Ltd, Elcograf S.p.A

The paper and board used in this book are made from wood from responsible sources

Hodder Children's Books
An imprint of
Hachette Children's Group
Part of Hodder & Stoughton
Carmelite House
50 Victoria Embankment
London EC4Y 0DZ

An Hachette UK Company
www.hachette.co.uk
www.hachettechildrens.co.uk

Contents

The Lost Motorcar 1
Loppy and the Witch 11
Mary, Mary, Quite Contrary 17
The Spick-and-Span Stone 25
He Couldn't Do It! 37
Betsy's Fairy Doll 55
The King's Treasure 69
The Dirty Old Hat 75
The Pinned-On Tail 85
Snippitty's Shears 95
The Good Luck Morning 105
Floppety Castle 115
The Wizard's Umbrella 125
My Goodness, What a Joke! 145

The Fairy and the Policeman 155
Who Came Creeping in the Door? 163
Roundy and the Keys 175
Mr Pink-Whistle is a Conjurer! 189
Tick-Tock's Tea Party 207
The Fly-Away Cottage 227
Winkle Makes a Mistake 249
The Little Clockwinder 261
'Tell Me My Name!' 267
Do Hurry Up, Dinah! 279
The Goblin Hat 293
Acknowledgements 303

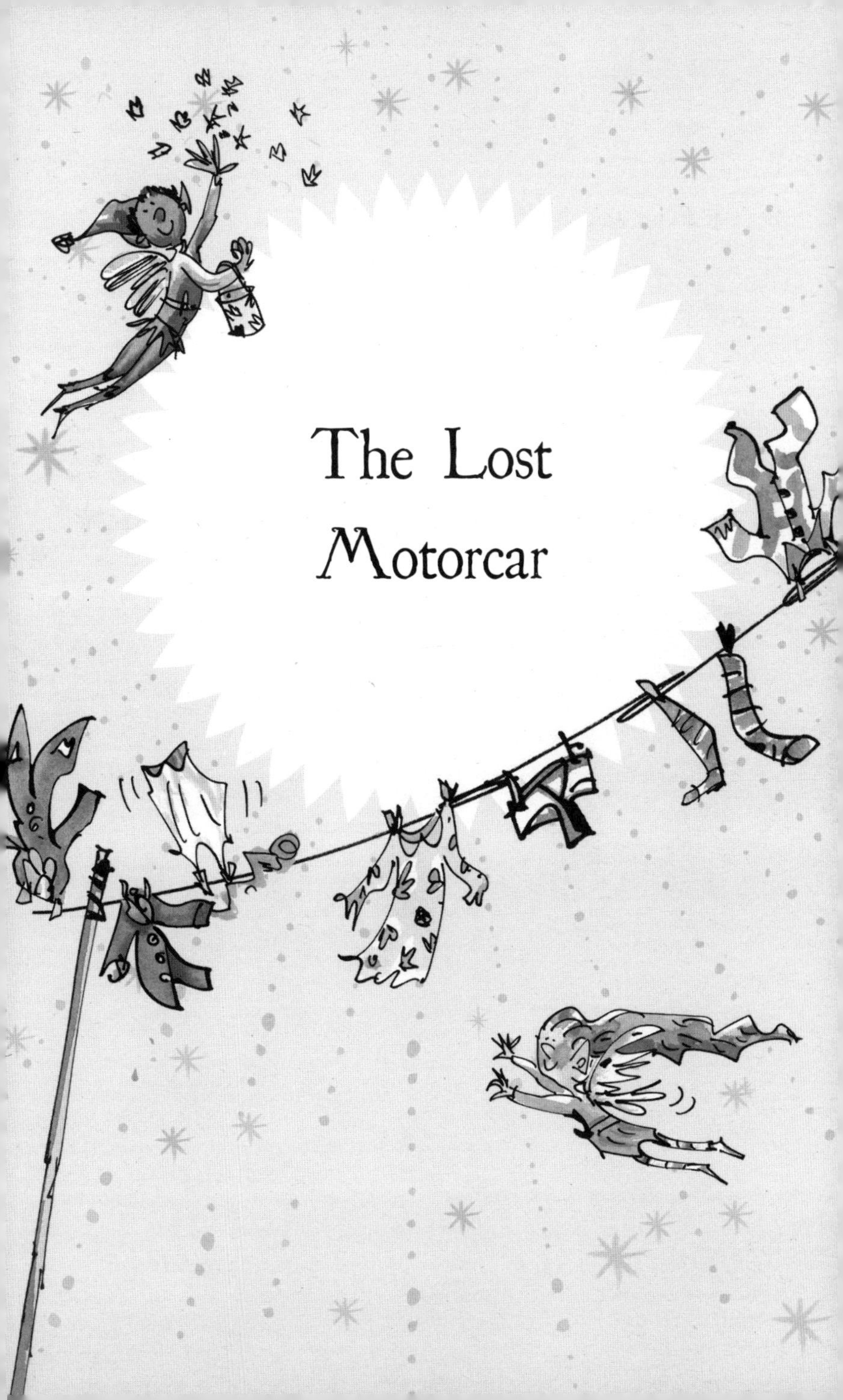

The Lost Motorcar

The Lost Motorcar

ONCE UPON A time, George had a toy motorcar that wound up with a little key. It was a yellow car, just big enough to take a little tin man to drive it and one passenger, who was usually somebody out of the Noah's ark.

One day George took the car out into the garden to play with. But it wouldn't run on the grass very well, even when it was fully wound up, so he left it there and went to fetch something else.

While he was in the house it began to rain and his mother called to him to stay in the nursery until the sun shone again. So George forgot about the toy car and left it out in the garden all day long.

The rain rained on it. Spiders ran all over it. An earwig thought it would make a nice hiding place and hid under the bonnet. A large fly crept there too.

George didn't remember that he had left it in the garden. He wanted to play with it in two days' time and he hunted in his toy cupboard for it – but of course it wasn't there. So he didn't bother any more, though he was sad not to have the little car, because it really was very nice indeed and could run at top speed twice round the nursery before it stopped.

The little yellow car lost all its bright paint in the next rainstorm. Red rust began to show here and there. Its key dropped out into the grass. The little tin man at the steering wheel split in half. One of the wheels came loose – so you can see that the toy car was in a very bad way.

And then one morning two little men with baskets came hurrying by. They were pixies, and not much bigger than your middle finger.

In their baskets were loaves of bread and cakes, for the two men were bakers and sold their goods to the little folk.

They suddenly saw the old toy motorcar and went up to it in surprise. 'What is it?' said Biscuit.

'It's a car!' said Rusky, his brother. 'An old toy car! Will it go?'

They pushed it – and it ran along on its four rusty wheels, though one wobbled a good bit, because it was so loose.

'It *does* go!' said Biscuit. 'I wonder who it belongs to.'

'I suppose it belongs to the little tin man at the wheel,' said Rusky. 'But he has split in half, so he's no use any more. I say, Biscuit – if only *we* could have this car! Think how we could take all our loaves and cakes round in no time. Our baskets are sometimes so heavy to carry and when it rains, they get wet. But if we had a car . . . !'

'Oh, Rusky! Do let's have it!' said Biscuit. 'We'll hurry along and deliver our things today, and then we'll come back and see what we can do with the car. It's just falling to pieces there, so we might as well have it for ourselves!'

Well, after about an hour the two little bakers came back. They pushed the car off to their tiny house under the hazel bush and then they had a good look at it.

'It wants a fine new coat of paint,' said Biscuit.

'It wants that wheel tightened,' said Rusky.

'It's got no key,' said Biscuit. 'How will it go?'

'We'll have to rub the wheels with a bit of Roll-Along Magic,' said Rusky, getting excited.

So they set to work. They took the poor little tin man away from the wheel. They screwed the loose wheel on tightly. And then they bought a tin of bright red paint and gave the whole car a beautiful coat of red.

'I think we'll paint the wheels yellow, not red,' said Biscuit. 'It would look more cheerful.'

So the wheels were painted yellow. Along the sides of the car the two bakers painted their names in yellow letters on the red – 'Biscuit and Rusky, Pixie Bakers'. When they had finished, the little toy car looked very smart indeed.

'Now for a bit of magic to rub on the wheels!' cried Rusky. So they got a bit of Roll-Along Magic and rubbed it on each of the four yellow wheels. Then in they got and drove the car off for its first spin.

It went at such speed! They tore round the garden path and back, and all the little folk came out in surprise to see them. And next day Biscuit and Rusky piled their bread and their delicious little cakes into the car, and drove off to deliver them to all their customers. It didn't take them nearly as long as usual and they were just as pleased as could be!

They even bought a tiny horn for the car that said 'honk-honk!' whenever a worm or a beetle ran across their path. And it was this horn that George heard one day when he was playing out in the garden near the hazel bush!

He heard the 'honk-honk!' and looked round to see

what could be making the noise. He suddenly saw the little red and yellow car rushing along, with Biscuit and Rusky inside, and he stared in such surprise that at first he couldn't say a word. Then he called out, 'I say! I say! Who are you? Stop a minute, do!'

The car stopped. Biscuit and Rusky grinned up at George. He stared down at the car. It looked like the one he had lost, but this was red with yellow wheels and his had been all yellow.

'That's a dear little car you've got,' he said. 'Where did you get it from?'

'We found it under there,' said Rusky, pointing. 'It belonged to a little tin man, who sat at the wheel, but he had split in half, so we took the car for ourselves and painted it brightly. Isn't it fine?'

'You know, it's *my* car!' said George, remembering the little tin man. 'It really is! I must have left it out in the garden. I'm sure I did!'

Biscuit and Rusky stared up at him in dismay. 'Oh, dear! Is it really your car? We do love it so – and you can't think how useful it is to us, because we use it to deliver our bread and cakes now, instead of carrying them over our shoulders in baskets. But, of course, if it's yours, you must have it back.'

They hopped out of the car, looking very sad and sorrowful. George smiled at them.

'Of course I shan't take it from you! I shouldn't have left it out in the garden. You've made it simply beautiful – and your names are on it too. You keep it. I'm very pleased to give it to you and I'll often be looking out for you. Do hoot your horn whenever you pass me, will you? Then I'll know you're there.'

Loppy and the Witch

Loppy and the Witch

THE QUEEN OF Fairyland was very much upset. The Green Witch had stolen from the palace a magic bag, a magic key and a magic jug, and nobody dared to try to get them back for fear that the witch would turn the pixie or elf who tried into a black beetle. Then who should put up his long-eared head but Loppy, the sandy rabbit!

'*I'll* get them back for you, Your Majesty!' he said. 'Goodbye!'

Off he went and stole into the Green Witch's cottage. She saw him and pounced on him. 'Ha!' she cried. 'I'll have you for dinner! Now I wonder what is the best way to cook a rabbit!'

'With onions!' said Loppy. 'I should taste fine with onions.'

'But I haven't any!' said the witch.

'I'll get some for you!' said Loppy. 'Can you lend me that bag to carry them in?'

The Green Witch was delighted to think of cooking onions with the rabbit, so she gladly gave Loppy the bag (which was the magic one, of course) and he ran off. But you may be sure he didn't go back with any onions! Not he! He gave the bag to the queen, and she was delighted.

Next day Loppy wandered into the witch's garden, and she caught hold of him by his long ears. 'Ha! I've got you again!' she cried. 'Why didn't you bring back those onions? I wish I could cook you for my dinner, but my fire is out and I haven't any sticks to light it with.'

'There are plenty at home in my woodshed,' said Loppy. 'But it's locked and I've lost the key. If you could lend me that key in your belt I believe it would unlock the door, and I could bring you back a bundle of sticks.'

The witch was pleased. She gave Loppy the key (which was the magic one, of course!) and he ran off. But you may be sure he didn't go back with any sticks! He gave the key to the queen.

Next day he went to the Green Witch's again and once more she caught him. 'I shan't let you go *this* time!' she said. 'I've got my fire going well, and I've plenty of onions. Ha, ha!'

'Yes, but have you any new milk to make nice rabbit gravy with?' asked Loppy. 'I shan't taste nice unless I'm cooked in milk.'

'No, I haven't,' said the witch, 'and the milkman doesn't call again today!'

'Well, lend me that blue jug over there and I'll go and buy two-penn'orth of fresh milk,' said Loppy. 'I shall taste beautiful then.'

So the witch gave him the blue jug (which was the magic one, of course!) and he ran off. But you may be sure be didn't come back with any new milk. Not he! He gave the jug to the queen.

'You shall be knighted for your bravery!' she cried. So Loppy became Sir Loppy the Sandy Rabbit, and very proud he was, as you can guess.

As for the Green Witch, she was so ashamed at having been tricked three times by a rabbit that she mounted her broomstick and flew away to the moon – and a very good thing too!

Mary, Mary, Quite Contrary

Mary, Mary, Quite Contrary

THERE WAS ONCE upon a time a little girl called Mary. She went to a school with other boys and girls, and because she was gentle, and they were rough, she used to get a great deal of teasing.

'Do you believe in fairies, Mary?' they asked one day.

'Of *course* I do!' said Mary in surprise.

'Oh, fancy! She believes in fairies! Isn't she a silly!' called the children, dancing round her in fun.

Mary went red, but just then the school bell rang, and all the children ran in.

One day, not long after, the teacher said she would

give a prize for the prettiest garden. The children could bring their own seeds and plant them in a corner of the garden, and look after them. Whoever had the prettiest garden should have a big, fat storybook for a prize.

The children were most excited.

'I shall plant poppies!' cried one, dancing off.

'I shall grow mignonette and candytuft,' sang another joyfully.

'What will you plant, Mary?' asked a third.

'I shall ask the fairies to give me some seeds!' said Mary.

'Oh Mary, Mary, quite contrary, ask a fairy, ask a fairy!' shouted the children rudely. 'Why don't you buy seeds like us? You never do as we do!'

Mary went to the fairies she knew, and asked for some seeds.

'Oh, dear! We've nothing that's any good for flowers!' said the fairies. 'We've given those to the gnomes to plant!'

Suddenly a little fairy laughed. 'Here's three bagfuls of pixie-seeds,' she said. 'The pixies grow the strangest things. Plant these, and see what happens. You won't get flowers, I'm afraid, but you may get something exciting!'

Mary took them and ran off. When she got to school next morning, she began to plant her seeds.

'Whatever seeds are you planting, Mary?' asked the children curiously. 'Oh, do look! She's got a bag full of the tiniest tiny shells! What is the good of planting those? *They'll* never grow!'

'And see!' cried another. 'Here's a bag of teeny-weeny things that look like bells! Oh Mary, Mary, quite contrary, you *are* silly!'

The third bag held curiously shaped and curiously coloured seeds, which looked like nothing in particular. Mary planted all three bagfuls of seeds in rows.

On the day of the prize giving, teachers and children flocked to the gardens to see who should win the prize. The little gardens were bright and colourful with roses and candytuft, poppies and snapdragons.

'Now let's go to Mary's garden!' laughed the children, running over into the corner where her garden was. There was Mary, looking in astonishment at it!

'Oh Mary, Mary, quite contrary, how does your garden grow?' cried the children.

Mary laughed a happy laugh, and clapped her hands.

'With silver bells, and cockle shells, and pretty maids all in a row!' she answered.

And sure enough she was right! For there grew a row of little green plants each with a silver bell swinging from it – and there grew a row of the finest, shiniest cockle shells – but best of all, there sat a row of the dearest, darlingest little girl dolls ever seen anywhere out of Fairyland!

'Pixie-seeds! Pixie-seeds!' cried Mary, dancing up

and down in delight, and laughing at the astonished faces of the children.

And, of course, you can guess whose garden won the prize, can't you?

The Spick-and-Span Stone

The Spick-and-Span Stone

ONCE THERE WAS a little gnome called Pinkie, who was always in a muddle. His bed was never made, his dishes were always dirty, his mats were full of dust and his garden was full of weeds. He could never find anything either. If he wanted the cloth to wipe up, he would spend an hour looking for it under all sorts of things. If he wanted to write a letter, he could never find his pen.

His neighbours were fed up, because when Pinkie really couldn't find something, he borrowed theirs, and lost that too, which was dreadfully annoying.

In the end, nobody took any notice of him. Nobody

asked him to parties. Nobody called on him. They weren't going to bother with an untidy little gnome any more. Pinkie was very miserable, and wondered what he could do about it.

Then one day he went for a walk and passed old Mother Bumble's cottage. She had been ill in bed, and now she was trying to put her cottage straight. Pinkie saw an odd person going up her front path. He was long and thin, with big flapping feet and a big nose. Mother Bumble seemed very pleased to see him and he went inside.

'That looks like the Flip-Flap Man,' said Pinkie. 'I wonder what he's gone to Mother Bumble's for?' He peeped in at the window and saw a curious sight. They were standing in the parlour, and on the table was a big yellow stone.

'That is my spick-and-span stone,' explained the Flip-Flap Man. 'Now, we'll soon get your cottage nice and tidy for you, Mother Bumble!'

He stroked the stone with his hands and sang in a

funny, high voice, 'Oh, spick-and-span stone, we'll leave you alone. And while we're away, work hard, I pray.' Then he and Mother Bumble went out. Pinkie watched them go.

Then he stared in surprise! For the spick-and-span stone swelled and hummed like a top. And all the dust on the table and chairs went rushing out of the window and past Pinkie's nose, and bits of fluff flew up the chimney, and the brass shovel and candlesticks suddenly shone dazzlingly bright, and the books all straightened themselves, and even the tablecloth pulled itself straight.

Pinkie's mouth fell so wide open that he nearly swallowed a pile of dust that came whisking out of the window. Then suddenly the spick-and-span stone became smaller and stopped humming. Its work was done. Everything was tidy.

Pinkie thought of his own untidy cottage, and how nobody was friends with him any more. He longed to have the spick-and-span stone.

But I know the Flip-Flap Man wouldn't lend it to me, he

thought. *Nobody lends me anything now. I'll borrow it without asking, and give it back afterwards.*

And the bad little gnome slipped in through the window, snatched the stone, and ran home with it without anyone seeing him. He put the spick-and-span stone on his untidy table and stroked it. Then he sang in a little high voice, 'Oh, spick-and-span stone, I'll leave you alone. And while I'm away, work hard, I pray.' He slipped out into the garden, and waited until the humming noise made by the stone stopped. Then he went indoors.

'Did ever you see such a lovely room!' he cried. 'Thank you, Spick-and-Span!'

He took it into his bedroom, and it did the same there. Then he put it in the garden, and it tidied up in a marvellous manner. Pinkie couldn't see how it was done, because things flew about so. He took it in, and put it on his mantelpiece.

'I don't think I'll return you just yet,' he said. 'I'll borrow you a bit longer.'

Now, that was being naughtier still, and Pinkie knew it. In the morning he got up late, and untidily got his breakfast. 'I needn't bother to wash up,' he said, grinning. 'Spick-and-Span will do it for me. It can make my bed too.' He put the stone on the table. 'Oh, spick-and-span stone, I'll leave you alone. And while I'm away, work hard, I pray.' Then he went out and waited.

It seemed to him that the stone hummed rather strangely – very high and shrill. *It sounds as if it were angry*, thought Pinkie uncomfortably.

When it stopped humming, he went into his kitchen. It was very tidy – very, very tidy. Pinkie was astonished. 'Where are my plates and cups?' he said. 'Where's my kettle? Where are my books? And where are my apples and sweets?'

Then he stared in surprise – for there they all were, stacked in a neat pile on a very high shelf that Pinkie never used.

'Bother!' he said. 'That's a silly trick. You've been a bit too tidy, Spick-and-Span! I'll take you back!' But the stone wasn't there. It was gone, and the table was bare!

'That's odd!' said Pinkie. 'I suppose it's gone back to the Flip-Flap Man.'

He went out to buy a ladder to reach the very high shelf. It cost him a lot of money, and he was very cross. When he got home, he took down all his things and put them in their proper places. The room looked so nice that Pinkie decided to go and ask Pippit, his neighbour, to come for tea. He got two cups and saucers out and a tin of cocoa, and he put the kettle on to boil. Then he ran to Pippit's house, and Pippit, having noticed Pinkie's tidy garden, decided Pinkie was trying to be good, and said he would come back with him.

Pippit was most surprised to find everything so tidy. But Pinkie was even more surprised at something. His cups and saucers, his kettle and the cocoa were gone! Quite gone! He couldn't think where to.

'Dear me, Pinkie, why ever do you keep all your things on that very high shelf?' Pippit said suddenly.

Pinkie looked up. There was everything, piled up on that shelf! And when he went to get them down he found his ladder was up on the shelf too! Dear, dear!

'I'll have to buy another ladder,' said Pinkie, rather frightened, and off he went, leaving Pippit to go back home again, very puzzled. Pinkie bought another ladder and hurried home. He climbed up it, and brought everything down again. And all the time Pinkie could hear a funny little humming noise!

That's the stone! he thought, *and it sounds like it's laughing at me! If only I could find it, I'd soon take it back!* But though he hunted everywhere, he couldn't find it. And everything kept vanishing to that very high shelf! If Pinkie left so much as a knife out of place, it would be gone next minute, and he'd have to climb up and get it. He had to make his bed too, because if he didn't the bedclothes would vanish to the shelf. He had never worked so hard, nor been so tidy, in his life before. And all the time he heard the stone laughing.

At last, when Pinkie had to buy a third ladder, because the other two were whisked up to the shelf again, the little gnome grew desperate. 'What shall I do?' he said groaning. 'The spick-and-span stone will ruin me.' He looked round his kitchen. Somewhere that stone was laughing. He could hear it, humming merrily.

'If only I could find you!' said Pinkie. 'You wouldn't be here a minute longer! But I don't dare to go to the Flip-Flap Man without you. He might turn me into a black beetle or something – and that would be dreadful!'

But the more he thought about it, the more he felt he ought to go and confess the naughty thing he had done. Besides, it was terrible to live with a magic stone; you never knew what it was going to do next. So Pinkie set out for the Flip-Flap Man's cottage. He knocked gently, and almost wished the Flip-Flap Man was not at home.

But the Flip-Flap Man opened the door, and Pinkie nervously told him what he had done. Pinkie cried and said he was very, very sorry indeed.

'And please, Mr Flip-Flap Man,' he begged, 'will you take your stone back?'

'All right,' said the Flip-Flap Man. 'I think you have learnt your lesson for taking it. But mind, Pinkie, even if I do take it back, it will leave its magic behind, and if you're untidy you may still find things flying up to that very high shelf!'

'I'll never be untidy again,' said Pinkie, and he really meant it.

The Flip-Flap Man went home with him. And there was the spick-and-span stone in the middle of Pinkie's kitchen table! The Flip-Flap Man put it in his pocket and said goodbye. Pinkie heard the stone humming loudly, as if it was very happy.

And after that Pinkie was as tidy as could be, and everyone was delighted. There was just one time that Pinkie was untidy – and that was the day he didn't brush his hair and had a hole in his stocking. What do you think happened? Why, he found himself whisked up on the shelf, and there he had to stay till Pippit called and got him down! I don't wonder he tries very hard to be tidy now, do you?

He Couldn't Do It!

He Couldn't Do It!

I REALLY MUST tell you how James Jonathan Brown got the better of a clever wizard called Mr Talk-a-Lot. It happened on a Saturday, when James had his weekly spending money in his pocket.

His father always gave him a shilling a week if his weekly school report was good. His mother gave him a shilling if he ran all her errands without grumbling, and his granny gave him sixpence a week simply because she loved him.

So that morning he had two shillings and a sixpence jingling in his pockets. He thought he would go to the farm over the hill, and buy some corn for his three hens, Hinny, Henny and Honey.

I'll go through the wood, he thought. *And I'll see if that funny little house is still there that I saw last time, almost hidden by trees. Nobody seems to know anything about it.*

So he went through the wood, and tried to find the little house. It had six chimneys, which James thought rather a lot for such a small cottage. *Six chimneys mean six fireplaces – and six fireplaces mean six rooms*, he thought. *And that cottage doesn't look as if it had more than two tiny rooms, at the most!*

He couldn't see the cottage anywhere – but he suddenly saw someone rushing through the trees at top speed, a bright red and black cloak sweeping behind him. *Now who's that?* thought James. *And why go about in fancy dress? I'll see where that fellow goes.*

He ran after the red and black cloak, which billowed as its owner sped along – and then James saw the little cottage with six chimneys that he had been looking for!

The red and black cloak disappeared in at the front door, and there came a loud slam.

Oh – so there's the cottage again – and that fancy dress person must be the owner, thought James. *Very interesting! If I believed in wizards and witches, which I don't, I might have thought that cloak belonged to one of them. Well – there's no harm in making a call!*

So he went to the little cottage and knocked sharply on the door. 'Who is it, bothering me this morning? Go away, I'm busy, I don't like visitors, they're a nuisance, for goodness' sake don't stand there, but . . .'

What a talker! thought James, and knocked loudly again. He called out at the top of his voice. 'May I have a drink of water, please?'

'Oh – it's a child, is it?' shouted the voice from inside. 'Well, you can come in! Wipe your feet please!'

And the door swung open, a long arm reached out, and there was James, feeling rather surprised, inside the little cottage. He had a great shock when he looked round!

'Good gracious – I thought this was a cottage – but it's *awfully* big!' said James, staring round a very big room indeed – so big that it had six fireplaces, one on each of its six sides. 'But – but, I say – how is it that it looks so small outside, and yet inside, it's . . .'

'Oh, don't talk so much,' said the person who had pulled him inside. He really was most extraordinary. He was very tall, wore a gleaming red cap, and had on the dazzling black and red cloak in which James had first seen him. His hands were never still, and his eyes shone as green as a cat's.

'I say, sir – what big green eyes you have!' said James in astonishment.

'Oh, don't speak to me as if you were Red Riding Hood speaking to the wolf!' said the green-eyed man. 'Haven't you seen a wizard before? Dear, dear, what in the world do they teach you at school these days? Now why do you want a drink of water? You're not thirsty. You're just inquisitive, you're . . .'

'Just stop talking for a minute, please,' said James,

rather alarmed at all this. 'Let me explain. I only want a . . .'

'Well, you don't. You never did,' said the wizard. 'By the way, my name's Talk-a-Lot. Don't tell me yours. I can see it written down in the notebook you carry in your pocket – James Jonathan Brown – what a name!'

'You surely can't see into my notebook when it's in my pocket!' said James, startled. 'Are you *really* a wizard? Do you do magic?'

'All day long! It's my hobby!' said Talk-a-Lot. 'I make magic and spells and wishing-wands, and now I'm trying to make dry water. Water's so *wet*, you know – all right when you want to have a bathe, but . . .'

'I think that's rather silly,' said James. 'Water's *always* wet. If it wasn't it wouldn't be water. Anyway, what would be the use of *dry* water?'

'Well, suppose you did your washing with dry water!' cried Talk-a-Lot. 'You wouldn't need to hang it out on the line to dry, would you? And just think of not having to wipe dishes and plates dry, or bothering to have towels to wipe your hands and face, or . . .'

'Please let me get a word in,' said James. 'I like magic as much as anyone, but not *silly* magic.'

The wizard was so angry when James said this, that he caught up a little sparkling wand and jabbed at him with it. 'I'll turn you into a hippopotamus, and send you to live in the wettest river that ever was,' he began. But James snatched the wand out of his hand.

'*I'll* have this!' he said. 'How many wishes will it make come true?'

'Only one,' said Talk-a-Lot. 'Put it down. You're a dangerous boy. All the same, I rather like you. Like to see me do a few tricks?'

'Well, yes, I would,' said James, still holding on to the little wand. 'Go ahead!'

'Tell me what you want me to do,' said Talk-a-Lot, 'but don't expect me to bring thunder and lightning down, and that sort of thing. I'm a bit scared of storms.'

'All right. See that teapot on the table?' said James. 'Make it hop into the air and pour out tea.'

Talk-a-Lot immediately began to sing out a string of magic words at the top of his voice, and as he went on and on, the teapot rose slowly into the air, swung across to James, and tipped itself over so that the spout poured warm tea all over him.

'Hey! I didn't say pour tea over *me*!' cried James, darting away. 'Don't be spiteful!'

'I'm not spiteful. I might have made the tea boiling hot, but I didn't,' said Talk-a-Lot. 'Teapot, sit down again. Well, what next, James Jonathan?'

'Er – let me see – make all your six fires die down a bit,' said James. 'This room's too hot.'

Talk-a-Lot at once began a kind of singsong again, magic words running off his tongue at top speed. And then, almost immediately, streams of water appeared in front of all six fireplaces and the fires sizzled loudly as the water poured over them. Black smoke billowed out into the room, and James began to cough.

'Stop the water!' coughed James. 'Quick!'

Talk-a-Lot waved his hands about and croaked out a few words. He was coughing too! The water disappeared, the smoke gradually went – and, of course, all the fires had gone out!

'Look at that – no fires!' cried the wizard. 'What a silly fellow you are! See what's happened now! I've a good mind to keep you here and make you light the fires and stoke them for me all day long! That's all a silly boy like you is any use for! Why did I say I liked you? I don't! You're a nuisance, and a . . .'

'Oh, stop *talking*!' said James. 'Don't you know enough magic to get those fires lit again without wood?'

'No, I don't,' said Talk-a-Lot sadly. 'I haven't come to the lesson on "How to Light Wet Wood" in my book of magic. It comes under the letter W right at the end of the book. Anyway, who are *you* to talk? I can do hundreds of things *you* can't do – and there isn't a single trick you can do that I couldn't do twice as quickly! Ha!'

'Ha to you!' said James. 'I bet I could do a trick that you couldn't do at all!'

'Go on then – do one! If you can do a trick I can't do at once, I'll – I'll – I'll . . .'

'You'll give me this little wishing-wand, with its one wish, for my own,' said James. 'Ha! You're afraid of saying you will, because you think I might know a trick that you *don't* know!'

'Rubbish! Nonsense! Foolish boy! Tell me the trick – and see me do it straight away!' cried the wizard, his eyes shining like a cat's at night.

'All right. I want a glass, please – that tumbler over there will do,' said James. Talk-a-Lot fetched it and put it on a table, that was covered with a green cloth. 'What next?' he said.

'We need a sixpence, and two shillings,' said James, and took his money out of his pocket. 'One or two pennies will do, but I haven't any.'

'You're not to use your own money – it might be magic,' said Talk-a-Lot fiercely.

'Don't be silly,' said James. 'I don't carry magic money about with me. I'm not a wizard! I'm a schoolboy. It's a trick I've often played on my friends at school. Now I'm going to play it on you!'

He placed his sixpence on the table, and put the glass over it, so that the coin was right in the middle. Then he took two separate shillings and put them under the rim of the upturned glass, so that the edge of the glass rested on them.

'There!' he said. 'See that? The little sixpence is in the middle, under the glass. The edges of the glass rest on the shillings, which are half under the glass and half outside. Now listen – *can you get that sixpence out from under the glass without touching either the shillings* or *the glass?'*

Talk-a-Lot stared at the glass and the three coins. He rubbed his chin. He frowned. 'I don't know the spell for that,' he said. 'But I expect I'll think of it.'

'You won't,' said James. 'Go on – try a few magic words. See what happens!'

Talk-a-Lot waved his hands about and muttered some strange-sounding words. The glass slowly changed to a bright green – but the sixpence still lay under it, unmoving.

'Hm!' said the wizard. '*That* spell's no good. I'll try another.' So he tried again, and the strange words he said made James feel quite shivery. He stared at the sixpence, wondering if such magic *might* move it out from under the glass. But no . . . it didn't move. All that happened was that the shillings turned black!

'You aren't using very clever magic,' said James scornfully.

'Well, what words do *you* say then, to get that sixpence out from under the glass, without touching either the coins or the glass?' asked Talk-a-Lot crossly. 'Tell me them, and I'll use them.'

'Right,' said James. 'Anything to help you! All I say is "Come along, little sixpence, come along! Come along to me!"'

'I don't believe it,' said Talk-a-Lot. 'But I'll try it.'

He waved his hand over the glass, and chanted loudly, 'Come along, little sixpence, come along! Come along to me!'

But the sixpence didn't move. It lay there, shining under the green glass, between the two black shillings.

James laughed. 'You might change the glass back to its right colour, and the shillings too,' he said. 'Then I'll show you how to do the trick. It's very, very simple.'

'If it was simple, I'd be able to do it,' said Talk-a-Lot sulkily. He muttered a few words, waved his hands, and the glass lost its green colour, and the shillings shone silver again.

'Thanks,' said James. 'Now watch. I'm going to say my own magic words, and just scrape the cloth with my finger like this. Very very magic, you know!'

And James bent over the table, put his hand down on the cloth near the edge of the glass, and began to scrape it sharply with his forefinger. As he scraped he chanted his own words.

'Come along, little sixpence, come along! Come along to me!'

And sure enough, the little sixpence moved under the glass, and over the cloth, and slipped out under the rim, between the two shillings! There it was, lying outside the glass – and James hadn't touched either the glass or the shillings – nor had he touched the sixpence!

'Wonderful!' said the wizard in amazement. 'Terrific! Marvellous! Where did you learn your magic?'

'From my granddad,' said James. 'He taught me this trick – and plenty of others too. Well – I'll be off now. Thanks for the wishing-wand!'

He picked up the wand, and Talk-a-Lot cried out at once. 'No, wait! I didn't think you'd do a trick I couldn't do! Wait! I *can't* give you that wand. There's still a wish left in it. How do I know what dreadful wish you'd wish? You might wish me away to the moon!'

'I might. But I shan't,' said James. 'I rather like you, you see, Talk-a-Lot. But I'll tell you what I *am* going to wish, if you like.'

'Yes. You tell me. I'd feel safer if you do,' said the wizard, looking quite worried.

'Well, I'm going home with it – and I'm going to wave it over my mother, and wish her a new washing machine,' said James. 'You're smiling! Well, I thought that would make you laugh! It'll make my mother laugh too – with joy! You've no idea how hard she has to work when she washes all my dirty things, and my brother's and sister's too. So *that's* what I'm going to use the wish for – I shouldn't *dream* of wasting it on you!'

'No. No, of course not,' said Talk-a-Lot. 'I see that now. But wishing-wands aren't usually used for washing machines, you know.'

'Well, there has to be a first time for everything,' said James, taking his sixpence and shillings off the table, and holding fast to the little wishing-wand.

'Goodbye, Talk-a-Lot. It's been a very pleasant morning.'

'Yes. It has,' said the wizard. 'I really do like you, Jonathan James. You might come and see me some time again. I *could* teach you a few magic tricks, you know.'

'Ha! You mean *I* could teach *you* some!' said James with a chuckle. 'All right – I'll be along some day. Meantime, you practise the magic trick *I* taught *you* – and don't forget the magic words!'

And away he went with the magic wand. What a wonderful surprise his mother is going to have!

As for the wizard, he is still practising the Sixpenny Trick! You can hear him any day saying, 'Come along, little sixpence, come along! Come along to me!'

You can do it too, you know. Try it, and astonish all your friends!

Betsy's Fairy Doll

Betsy's Fairy Doll

IT ALL BEGAN on a day when Betsy was walking with her doll's pram by the big pond at the end of the lane. She was going along by herself, thinking of the delicious ginger buns that her mother had promised to make her for tea – and suddenly she heard a splash, and saw some big ripples on the pond.

Something's fallen in! she thought to herself, and she stopped in surprise and looked. At first she couldn't see anything at all in the pond, but then she saw a tiny little thing which was bobbing about a good way out in the middle.

Whatever could it be?

Then Betsy heard a little high voice. 'Help! Help!'

'Gracious, whatever is it?' wondered Betsy in alarm. She quickly broke a long twig off a nearby bush and tried to reach out to the little bobbing thing with it – and to her enormous surprise the thing clung on to it at once!

'Pull me in, pull me in!' she heard it cry. So she pulled the twig and then found that holding tightly to the end of it was – whatever do you think! – a little dark-haired fairy, with wet, bedraggled wings, looking very frightened and cold.

'Oh, thank you, thank you so very much!' said the little creature. 'You saved my life! I was talking to Bushy the squirrel up in the tree there and I seem to have lost my balance and fallen into the water.'

'How are you going to get dry?' asked Betsy, gazing in surprise at the wet fairy. 'You do look so wet and cold.'

'I don't know,' said the fairy. 'But perhaps I can fly off somewhere and dry myself with a dead leaf.'

She tried to spread her dripping wings – and then she gave a cry of dismay.

'Oh! My wings are hurt! They are all bent! I shall have to grow new ones before I will be able to fly again. Whatever shall I do?'

Then Betsy had a splendid idea. She clapped her hands at the thought of it.

'Oh, do come home with me,' she begged. 'I have a dear little doll's house with a nice bed in it where you can sleep. I have lots of doll's clothes that would fit you perfectly, and there's a lovely doll's bath you can wash in. You could live with me till your wings have grown again. Do say you will! It would be so lovely for me, because I haven't any brothers or sisters, and I'd love to have a fairy to play with.'

'It really is very kind of you,' said the fairy, shivering. 'Are you sure I shan't be in the way? You won't tell anybody about me, will you?'

'Of course I won't,' said Betsy. 'It will be a real

secret. I'm very good at keeping secrets, you know. And you won't be in the way at all – I'd simply love to have you.'

'*A-tishoo, a-tishoo*!' sneezed the fairy suddenly.

'Oh, dear, I think you must be catching cold already!' cried Betsy. 'Quick, wrap this doll's shawl round you and I'll put you in the pram and wheel you home to my bedroom. There's a lovely fire there.'

The fairy wrapped the woolly shawl round her and then Betsy lifted the little creature into the pram. She hurried home, and when at last she was safely in her own bedroom she took out the fairy and stood her in front of the fire.

'Take off your wet clothes,' she said to the fairy. 'I'm going to find some nice warm ones out of my doll's wardrobe. I've some that will just fit you.'

The fairy slipped off her wet clothes, and dried herself on a little towel that Betsy gave her. Then she dressed herself in the doll's clothes, which fitted her really beautifully. The dress was pale blue and the stockings and shoes matched. The fairy thought she looked very nice.

'What is your name?' asked Betsy. 'Mine's Betsy.'

'Mine is Tippitty,' said the fairy. 'I say, would you mind terribly finding some scissors so that you can clip off my wings for me, please?'

'Clip off your wings!' said Betsy in great surprise. 'But whatever for?'

'Well, my new ones won't grow till the old ones are clipped off,' said Tippitty. 'It won't hurt me. Just take your scissors and cut them off, please.'

So Betsy took the scissors from her sewing box and clipped the fairy's wings off. It seemed such a pity, but still, if new ones would grow soon, perhaps it didn't matter. Betsy put the clipped-off wings into a box to keep. They were so pretty – just like a butterfly's powdery wings.

'I'd better pretend to be one of your dolls if anyone comes in,' said Tippitty, doing up her blue shoes. 'Listen! Is that someone coming now?'

'Yes, it's Auntie Jane coming to tell me it's time for tea,' said Betsy. 'Daddy is out today, so we're having our tea early.'

The door opened and Auntie Jane came in.

'Mummy wants you to come down to tea now,' she said. 'Hurry up, because there are ginger buns for you.'

Betsy looked at the fairy. She had made herself stiff and straight, just like a doll. Nobody would know she was a fairy and not a doll.

'Tell Mummy I'm just coming,' said Betsy. She washed her hands, brushed her hair, told the fairy to keep warm by the fire, and then went downstairs to have tea.

'Mummy, may I have some milk, some biscuits and a ginger bun?' asked Betsy when she had finished her tea. 'I want to play with my doll's tea set.'

'Yes, dear,' said Mother. 'Take what you want. I will come up to you at bedtime. Play quietly till then.'

Betsy was pleased. She took the jug of milk, four biscuits and a bun. Then off she ran upstairs. The fairy was still by the fire, looking much better, though she still kept sneezing.

Betsy got out her tea set and poured the milk into the teapot. She put the biscuits on a plate and the bun on another plate. Then she called the fairy to have her tea.

The cup was just the right size for her to drink from, and she was very pleased. She ate a good tea and then Betsy said she had better go to bed in case her cold got worse.

It was just like having a real live doll. Betsy brushed the fairy's long dark hair, and then told the fairy she could wash in the doll's bath if she liked.

There was one bed in the doll's house which was much bigger than the rest. The fairy climbed into that and Betsy covered her up and tucked her in.

'I'm so sleepy,' said Tippitty, yawning. 'I think I shall soon be asleep.'

'I'll sing you to sleep,' said Betsy. So she sang all the nursery rhymes she knew in a soft little voice, and very soon the fairy was fast asleep. Betsy shut the front of the doll's house just as her mother came up to say it was bedtime. She longed to show her mother the fairy in the doll's bed but it was a secret and so she couldn't.

Tippitty lived with Betsy for three weeks, until her new wings grew. At first she kept them neatly folded under her dress, but when they grew larger Betsy cut a hole in the blue dress and the wings grew out of the hole. It was most exciting to watch them.

Betsy took Tippitty out in her doll's pram each day for a walk. She gave her her meals out of the doll's cups and dishes. She played with her and told her stories. The fairy thought she had never ever met such a nice little girl in all her life.

At last the time came for Tippitty to go. Her new wings had quite grown and were beautiful. The fairy could fly well with them, and there was no need for her to stay with Betsy any longer.

But she was very sorry to go – and as for Betsy, she

couldn't bear to think that she wouldn't have her small playmate any longer. She cried when the fairy said she must say goodbye.

'You have been so good and kind to me, Betsy,' said Tippitty. 'Is there anything I can do for you? Anything at all?'

'I suppose you couldn't give me a baby brother or sister, could you?' asked Betsy. 'It's so lonely being the only child. I haven't anyone to play with or love. I wish I could have a baby brother or sister!'

'I'll see what I can do for you,' promised Tippitty. She kissed Betsy, spread her wings, and flew to the window. 'I'll come back and see you sometimes,' she said, and off she went.

Betsy was very lonely when she was gone. She often took out the box in which she had put the clipped-off wings, and looked at them, wishing and wishing that Tippitty would come back and live with her.

And then one morning a wonderful thing happened.

Auntie Jane came to her room and woke her up, and said, 'Betsy, just fancy! You've got a little baby brother! He came in the night!'

Betsy sprang up in bed in delight. So her wish had come true! Oh, how perfectly lovely! She wasn't going to be an only child any more – the fairy had granted her wish.

'Oh, I wish we could call the baby Tippitty!' said Betsy. 'Do you think Mummy would agree, Auntie Jane?'

'Goodness me, whatever for?' asked Auntie Jane in astonishment. 'I never heard such a name before. What put it into your head, child?'

But Betsy wouldn't tell her. The baby was called Robin, and Betsy loved him very much – far more than she had loved Tippitty. Her mother soon let her hold him and carry him, and one evening she even let Betsy bath him.

Tippitty happened to look in at the window just as Betsy was bathing the baby – but Betsy didn't even see her. She was far too happy. Tippitty smiled and flew away.

'Betsy will never miss me now!' she said. 'She's got somebody better!'

The King's Treasure

The King's Treasure

ONCE UPON A time the king of Cuckoo Wood had a treasure he wanted to hide. So he hunted about and at last found a hole under the roots of an old tree. Into this hole he pushed his treasure, and left it there thinking himself to be quite unseen.

But Green-Eyes the gnome saw him. Green-Eyes was afraid to get the treasure from the hole himself, for he feared the king's anger when he found out – so he made up his mind to sell his secret to the Grumpy Witch, who would, no doubt, pay him much gold for it. He waited until the king had gone, and then he slipped from his hiding place and ran to the old tree.

A primrose root grew by it and he bent down and nicked a little piece from the edge of each yellow petal, so that he might know the place again by the marked primrose.

Then off he went to see the Grumpy Witch. Her eyes gleamed when she heard his news, for she guessed that the king's treasure was his magic wand which she longed to use.

'You will know the place by a certain primrose root,' said Green-Eyes. 'I nicked a piece out of each yellow petal, so that you might know that the tree by which it grew was the one under which the treasure was hidden.'

Off went the witch and the first thing she saw when she reached the wood was a primrose root and each of the flowers had a piece nicked out of the edge of its petals. Eagerly she dug around the tree, but no treasure did she find – and then, hearing loud laughter, she looked up to see a crowd of elves jeering at her. 'Seek for another primrose!' they cried. She looked around – and saw that every primrose was marked the same! The elves had seen Green-Eyes' trick and had done the same to each primrose in the wood! In anger the witch went away and bade Green-Eyes watch to see where the treasure was once more.

He did so – and when he saw the king visiting the tree again, he took out his knife and cut a tiny circle at the top of an ivy berry growing on the ivy that climbed around the tree. By that little cut circle the witch would know the tree.

But alas for her! When she went to seek the marked berry to find the treasure, she saw that every berry on every ivy plant was cut in the same way! And once more she heard the elves laughing loudly, and knew that they had cleverly tricked her by marking each berry in the wood in the same way as Green-Eyes had marked his! Then in a rage she rushed back to the gnome, turned him into a snake, which suited his nature very well, and gave up all hope of finding the treasure.

When the elves told the king what they had done

he laughed in delight. 'A clever trick!' he said, and went to see the primroses and the ivy berries.

'They shall always be marked in this way!' he cried. 'And that will be a warning to wicked gnomes not to meddle with things that belong to others.'

And the strange thing is, boys and girls, that every primrose still shows the little nick in the edge of each petal, and every ivy berry still has a tiny circle cut in the top. Find some and see if you can draw them to show their magic marks!

The Dirty Old Hat

The Dirty Old Hat

ONCE FLIBBERTY WENT to have a cup of tea in Dame Trotty's tearoom. It was crowded with people, for Dame Trotty made lovely buns and biscuits.

Flibberty sat down, after he had hung his hat up on the peg behind him. He ordered tea and cakes, and enjoyed his tea very much.

Then he stood up, took down what he thought was his hat from the peg behind, and went out. But it wasn't his hat. It was the Little Enchanter's hat and it was a magic one. It looked dirty and old, but it was crammed full of magic.

Flibberty put the hat on and went out, humming.

He wished it wasn't such a long way home. He looked down at his shoes and sighed.

'You're uncomfortable shoes,' he said. 'You're too small. I wish I had lovely red ones, like the ones Prince Twinkle has.'

To his enormous astonishment his old shoes disappeared, and he saw on his feet a pair of fine red leather ones. Flibberty couldn't believe his eyes!

'Look at that now!' he said. 'A pair of new shoes – and all for the wishing! There must be something magic about me today!'

He stood still and thought for a moment. Then he wished again. 'I'd like a red cloak like Prince Twinkle's too,' he said. And at once a red cloak swung out from his shoulders! Flibberty was so delighted he couldn't say a word for quite two minutes.

'I'm grand!' he said. 'Red shoes and red cloak! Would you believe it! I'll wish for a few more things!'

He wished for a stick with a gold handle. It came into his hand at once. Marvellous!

'This wishing business is a very good thing!' said Flibberty, pleased. 'I'll have a new suit now – gold and silver, please, with shining buttons all the way down!' It came, of course! Flibberty really did look very grand now. He thought he would like a carriage of his own.

'I know what I'll do! I'll wish for a carriage and go and call on Gibberty in it!' he said. Gibberty was his friend. They lived together. How surprised Gibberty would be to see Flibberty arriving in a carriage, all dressed up like a prince!

'I wish for a carriage!' said Flibberty. One appeared at once – but it was too small for Flibberty and had no horses.

'I wish for a *big* carriage, and twelve white horses,' he said grandly. They were there! The white horses pawed the ground and one of them neighed.

'They're absolutely real!' said Flibberty. He climbed up into the coachman's seat and then decided that there were too many horses for him to drive. So he got down and climbed into the carriage instead. Then he wished for two coachmen and two footmen. 'I'll have them dressed in red and silver,' he said.

They appeared, dressed in red and silver. Flibberty couldn't help feeling delighted with himself. He hoped he would meet plenty of people on the way home. Wouldn't they stare to see him in his lovely carriage with coachmen and footmen!

I'll have some dogs too, he suddenly thought. *I like dogs. I'll have about a hundred, and they can run behind the carriage.*

'I wish for a hundred dogs, please,' he said out loud. The dogs appeared. They seemed very well-behaved. They didn't jump up and try to lick Flibberty. They put themselves behind the carriage, and not one of them barked.

Flibberty half thought he would have some cats as well, just to make a sensation, but he decided he wouldn't. It might make the dogs ill-behaved if he made cats run with them.

And now I think I'll have a sack of gold pieces and throw

them out as I go along, thought Flibberty. *That would be a kind and princely thing to do! I wish for a sack of gold!* It appeared on the seat beside him. Ah, that was fine. Now he would drive slowly along to his house, and wouldn't he enjoy seeing Gibberty's face when he came to the door!

'Drive on!' he commanded the coachmen, and on they drove. The horses' hooves made a tremendous noise, clip-clopping along. People came out to see them. When they saw the beautiful carriage and horses, and all the dogs following behind, they stared as if they couldn't believe their eyes!

They didn't even recognise Flibberty! He bowed and smiled to them, but not one of them guessed this grand prince to be the little Flibberty they knew so well. He put his hand into the sack and drew out a dozen gold pieces. He threw them to the delighted people.

This will make them rich! thought Flibberty, pleased. *There's Dame Crick – she's picked up three gold pieces! My, my, won't she be glad!*

Soon he arrived at his cottage. Gibberty, hearing the noise of the horses, came running out. He didn't recognise Flibberty at all. He bowed very low indeed.

'Gibberty! It's me, Flibberty!' said his friend with a chuckle. Gibberty looked up in great astonishment. Yes – it *was* Flibberty. Well, well, well!

'Whatever's happened to you?' said Gibberty.

'I don't know,' said Flibberty. 'It must be my lucky day, I should think. Everything I wish for comes true. It's marvellous.'

'Well, wish something for *me*, quick!' said Gibberty.

'Wait a bit, wait a bit! Don't rush me so,' said Flibberty. 'You haven't admired my twelve white horses and my hundred dogs.'

'I can't imagine why you wished for a hundred dogs,' said Gibberty, who wasn't very fond of dogs. 'I don't know how we're going to feed them, or where they'll live.'

'I shall wish them magnificent kennels and stacks of the most wonderful food,' said Flibberty.

'Well, wish some wonderful food for me this very minute,' said Gibberty. 'I'm hungry! Come on, Flibberty, use some of your magic for *me*!'

'I'll wish you a fine suit of clothes, like mine,' said Flibberty.

'Well, don't wish me a hat like yours!' said Gibberty. 'I never saw such a dirty old thing in my life! Why don't you wish for a new one?'

Flibberty took his hat off his head and looked at it in surprise. 'It's not mine,' he said. 'What a dirty old hat! How disgusting! I shan't wear it. I shall throw it away!' He threw it high in the air. It caught on a tree – and just as it left Flibberty's hand, everything that he had wished for disappeared! His new clothes went, his carriage, horses, servants and dogs! Nothing was left at all!

'They've gone!' said Flibberty. 'Oh, you silly creature, Gibberty! The magic must have been in that hat! Quick, we must get it down from that tree.' But before they could get it down the Little Enchanter came hurrying along to get it. He had heard of Flibberty's good luck and had guessed what had happened! Flibberty had taken his hat by mistake.

'That's *my* hat!' he roared, and he threw Flibberty's at him. 'Here's yours. You leave my hat alone! If you've used up all the magic in it I'll turn you into a scrubbing brush and use you for spring-cleaning!'

'Ooooh!' squealed Flibberty and Gibberty and they tore indoors. But luckily Flibberty hadn't used all the magic, and the Little Enchanter put his hat firmly on his head and strode off home.

'To think I wore a wishing-hat and didn't know it but threw it away!' groaned Flibberty. 'Next time I'll be a lot more careful!'

I daresay he will – but there won't *be* a next time!

The Pinned-On Tail

The Pinned-On Tail

THE PINK MONKEY had a very long tail – but do you know he had to keep it *pinned* on because it was loose and fell off if he didn't.

Poor monkey! He was very sad about this. You see, he was a grand monkey indeed, bright pink, with a brown nose, green eyes and paws very like hands – but his pinned-on tail spoilt him.

But what was he to do about it? He didn't want it sewn on, because he felt sure it would hurt him. He did once borrow some glue and try to stick it on – but unfortunately he got the glue all over himself, and stuck *both* ends of his tail on – one to his back and the other to his front – so that was worse than ever.

He also sat down on a piece of newspaper while he was trying to glue himself, and when he got up, he had stuck to the paper – so for a long time he had to walk about with sheets of paper behind him until the teddy bear kindly offered to try to get it off.

It hurt a bit – but at last the monkey was quite free of all the newspaper. The teddy bear wrapped it up and was just going to throw it into the fire when the monkey gave a scream.

'Teddy! You've pulled my tail away too – don't throw it into the fire!'

The teddy opened the newspaper – and there was the tail, all screwed up too! The monkey pounced on it and took it.

'Ooh! It nearly went into the fire. Teddy, where is there a safety pin? An ordinary pin is no use.'

Teddy went to Nurse's workbasket and took out a big safety pin. The monkey screwed himself round and pinned on his long woolly tail. He wouldn't let the teddy do it in case it hurt him.

'It's crooked,' said Teddy.

''Tisn't,' said the monkey, trying to look over his shoulder at his tail.

''Tis!' said the teddy.

'Well, I *like* it crooked,' said the monkey. But he didn't like it crooked. He didn't like it pinned on at all. It did spoil his beauty so. He looked quite all right from the front – but from behind he looked dreadful – all safety pin and crooked tail.

One night he thought he would creep out and go to the little old woman who lived under the hedge nearby. People said she was very clever. The monkey felt sure she was clever enough to fix his tail on without glue or pins.

So off he went. The moon shone down on his safety pin and made it very bright. He hunted about for the little old woman, but he couldn't seem to find her house.

Then suddenly he heard a shout for help.

'Quick! Help me! Help me!'

Monkey ran on all fours to the place where the shouting came from. He was just in time to see a small elf getting up off the ground – and a frog hopping away fast with something in his front paws.

'What's the matter?' asked the monkey.

'Oh, that horrid, horrid frog has stolen my lovely shawl,' sobbed the elf. 'I shall get cold! I'm going to a party, and I shall get so hot dancing – and then I shall get a chill afterwards. I always do if I have no scarf or shawl. Oh, I'm so sad!'

'Can't you go home and borrow a scarf?' said the monkey, feeling sorry for the pretty little elf.

'My home is ever so far away,' said the elf, drying her eyes and looking at the monkey. Then she saw his long woolly tail, which he had curled round his waist for the moment. She pointed to it.

'Oh, Monkey! If you'd lend me that lovely woolly thing you've got round your waist I could wrap it round my throat and use it for a scarf. Then I wouldn't get cold.'

'But that's my *tail*,' said the monkey, offended.

'Oh, is it?' said the elf. 'Why don't you let it go loose then? It seems funny to tie it round your waist.'

'Well, I tie it round because it's only pinned on,' said the monkey. 'And you see, if the pin came undone I might lose my tail and not know it.'

'Only *pinned* on!' shrieked the elf. 'Well, unpin it then and lend it to me, can't you? It would make such a *lovely* scarf. Oh dear, darling, beautiful Monkey, unpin your tail and lend it to me, do, do, do!'

The elf flung her arms round the surprised monkey – and she was so sweet and so loving that he simply couldn't say no to her. So he solemnly unpinned his tail, took it off and handed it to her. The elf wrapped it round her neck and danced in delight. 'It's warm, warm, warm!' she sang. 'Come on, Monkey darling – come with me to the party!'

And, to the pink monkey's great astonishment, the

elf dragged him through the hedge – and there he was at the party! You should have seen the fairies, magical brownies, elves, gnomes and pixies there! Hundreds of them, all chatting and laughing and dancing. When they saw the elf with the pink monkey they crowded round in surprise. The monkey blushed pinker than ever.

'I don't like being here without my tail,' he whispered to the elf. 'I don't feel dressed.'

'Don't be silly!' said the elf. 'Oh, listen, everyone, I've had an adventure! A frog stole my shawl – and I met this monkey who had a *pinned*-on tail – and he unpinned it and gave it to me for a scarf!'

'Three cheers for good old Monkey!' cried all the fairies and they swung Monkey round and round till he felt quite giddy. Nobody seemed to mind him not having a tail. The elf took it off when she danced and put it on a chair. Monkey kept his eyes on it, because he didn't want it to be lost. The next time the little elf put it round her neck, he went up to her and told her how he had meant to go to the old woman who lived under the hedge and ask her to fix it on properly for him.

'Poor old Monkey!' said the elf, patting his big nose. 'Don't you worry about that. I know enough magic for that!'

'*Do* you!' said Monkey in surprise.

'Of course!' said the elf. 'Look – the party is nearly over. I can borrow a shawl to go home in. You can have your tail back – and we'll fix it on properly for you – without a pin or anything.'

She clapped her hands and a dozen little folk danced up to her. She told them what she wanted, and they made a circle with the monkey in the middle. They all danced round, singing a little magic song – and then the elf threw the tail straight at Monkey's back – and lo and behold, it stuck there, in exactly the right place! Fancy that!

'It's on, it's on!' shouted Monkey, tugging at it in delight to make sure. 'Oh, thank you a hundred times, little elf.'

The elf hugged him. 'You're a darling,' she said. 'I'm pleased to have done you a good turn. I did love wearing your warm tail for a scarf. I might come and borrow it again – you never know!'

Monkey went home as happy as could be. And *how* all the toys stared when he showed them his tail and told them his adventures. He *was* proud of having a tail that had been a scarf, I can tell you!

Snippitty's Shears

Snippitty's Shears

SNIPPITTY'S GARDEN WAS in a dreadful mess. The grass wanted cutting, the hedge wanted clipping, and the weeds had grown so tall that Snippitty could hardly see the flowers.

He had been away on his holiday, and he was very cross to see how untidy his garden was.

I don't feel like spending all the week clipping and cutting, he thought. *I think I'll go to Puddle the gnome and buy a pair of magic shears. Then they can do the work, and I shall be able to sit in the sunshine and read my newspaper.*

So he went to Puddle's shop. It was a curious shop, hung with all kinds of things, from pins to balloons.

Puddle was very clever, and he could put a spell into anything and make it very powerful indeed.

'I want a pair of shears with a cutting spell in them,' said Snippitty, when he walked inside the shop.

'Here's a fine pair,' said Puddle, taking down a glittering pair of sharp-looking shears.

'How much?' asked Snippitty.

'Five shillings,' said Puddle.

'Don't be foolish,' said Snippitty. 'That's far too much.'

'It isn't, and you know it isn't,' said Puddle indignantly. 'Why, you couldn't buy these shears at even ten shillings in the next town. They would be quite fifteen shillings.'

Snippitty knew that that was true. Puddle's shears were very good indeed, and the magic in them made them powerful. But he was a mean little fellow, and he wasn't going to pay more than he could help.

'I'll give you three shillings for them,' he said, getting out his purse.

'No,' said Puddle.

'Yes,' said Snippitty. 'Not a penny more.'

'No, I tell you,' said Puddle. 'Why, they cost more than that to make.'

'I don't believe you,' said Snippitty rudely.

Puddle looked at the mean little gnome and felt very angry.

'All right,' he said suddenly with a grin. 'You can have them for three shillings.'

Snippitty smiled in delight to think that he had got his way. He paid out the money, took the shears and went off with them.

He stuck them in the grass and said loudly, 'Shears, do your work!'

At once the shears began cutting the grass very closely and evenly. Snippitty watched them, pleased to think that he could sit down and read while his shears did all his work.

When the shears had finished cutting his lawn, Snippitty saw them fly across to the privet hedge and begin to clip that. He was delighted to see what a fine job they made of the hedge.

'I'll just finish this story in my paper and then set the shears to work on those tall weeds,' said Snippitty. So he settled down comfortably to his reading – but, dear me, his chair was so soft and the sun was so warm that Snippitty fell fast asleep!

He slept on and on – and the shears went on and on working. They finished the hedge and looked round for something else to clip. They flew across to the weeds and cut those down too. Then they clipped down all the rose trees that Snippitty was so proud of, and looked round for something else.

Clip! The clothes-line was cut in half and all the clothes fell to the ground. The shears soon cut them up into little pieces, and then looked round again.

Clip! Down came the tennis net, and was soon cut into tiny little pieces on the lawn. What next? Ha, there was Snippitty lying fast asleep in the sunshine, his long white beard reaching almost down to his knees.

The shears flew over to him. Clip! Clip! Clip! The beard that Snippitty was so proud of was cut into three pieces, and the shears began to clip it very small. The noise woke Snippitty, and he sat up and yawned.

But, oh, my goodness, when he saw what the shears had done, he shouted in dismay.

'Stop! Stop! Oh, you wicked shears, look what you've done! You've taken off my beautiful beard! You've chopped my clothes-line in half! You've cut down my rose trees! You've ruined my tennis net! Oh, oh, stop, I tell you, stop!'

But nothing would stop those shears! They rushed at Snippitty and cut off the points of his shoes. Then they snipped all the buttons off his tunic and clipped the point off his hat. Snippitty gave a yell and rushed up the road to Puddle's shop. He burst in at the door and closed it behind him.

'Good gracious, Snippitty, whatever's the matter?' asked Puddle.

'It's those shears!' said Snippitty, almost crying.

'They've got a spell to make them work, but not one to make them stop. Put it in at once, Puddle. Look what they've done to my lovely beard!'

Puddle laughed till the tears rolled down his long nose and dropped on the counter with a splash.

'If you want another spell, it will be two shillings extra,' he said. 'I told you those shears were five shillings, you know. You only paid me three shillings and surely you didn't expect to get such a lot for your money. Will you pay me two shillings more, and I will put a stop-spell in the shears?'

Snippitty opened his purse and put two shillings on the counter.

'I have been mean,' he said. 'And I am well punished. Here is your money. Take it.'

Puddle took it, and then opened the door. The shears flew in and Puddle chanted some magic words. In a trice the shears fell to the counter and lay there quite still.

Snippitty picked them up and shook them.

'You wicked things!' he cried. 'You've done pounds' worth of damage! I'll throw you away!'

'Don't do that,' said Puddle. 'They might come in useful next year.'

'So they might,' said Snippitty with a sigh and put them under his arm. 'Well, I'm going back to clear up all the damage. Good day to you, Puddle. I shan't be mean again. It certainly doesn't pay.'

And I quite agree with him, don't you?

The Good Luck Morning

The Good Luck Morning

THE GOOD LUCK Morning began quite suddenly. It happened when Toppy was coming back from taking a message for his aunt. He was skipping along merrily, and was just bending down to take a stone out of his shoe, when he saw a book lying on the ground.

He forgot about the stone in his shoe and picked up the book. Inside was written, 'This book belongs to Dame Spillikins.'

'I'll take it over to her,' said Toppy, and went off to her cottage. 'She must have dropped it.'

Dame Spillikins was simply delighted to have her book back. 'Why, it's my book of spells, Toppy!' she said. 'You're sure you haven't peeped inside and read some of them?'

'No, ma'am, of course not,' said Toppy.

'I've just baked some meat pies,' said Dame Spillikins, turning to her oven. 'You sit down for a minute, Toppy, and I'll give you one for your kindness.' Toppy sat down, beaming. 'I'm in luck!' he said to the lady. 'I really am.'

He ate the warm meat pie, and finished every crumb. 'Most delicious!' he said to Dame Spillikins. 'Thank you very much. Now I must be getting along.'

So off he went. Before very long he saw Mother Fly-Around. She had a magic broomstick that was the envy of everyone in the town. She didn't bother about buses or trains – she just sat on her broomstick, told it where to go, and it went.

Toppy had always longed for a ride on the wonderful broomstick, but he had never had one. He watched Mother Fly-Around land in her garden and get off the broomstick – and then he saw that she had dropped her shopping basket, and everything had rolled out.

He ran in at the gate at once. 'I'll pick them up for you, Mother Fly-Around. Don't you worry!'

And in a second, he had picked everything up and popped it back into her basket. Mother Fly-Around was pleased.

'You're a nice, good-mannered creature,' she said to Toppy. 'Would you like a little ride on my broomstick?'

Well! Toppy could hardly believe his ears. Why, Mother Fly-Around *never* lent her broomstick to anyone. What a bit of luck!

'Oh, yes, *please*,' said Toppy, thrilled, and he got on it, riding it astride like a horse. 'Take me to the market and back!' he ordered, and at once the stick rose into the air and made off to the market. It was the loveliest feeling Toppy had ever had in his life, riding a broomstick!

This is certainly my Good Luck Morning, he thought. *Hey, broomstick, you're going a bit too fast. Whoooooosh!*

Down he went again to Mother Fly-Around's. 'Thank you very much,' he said. 'I did enjoy that.'

Off he went again, on his way back to his aunt's. Soon he met Twinkles carrying a large box of chocolates.

'Hallo, Toppy,' said Twinkles. 'Look what my uncle has given me! Take three!'

'Oooooh!' said Toppy, as Twinkles took off the lid and showed rows of enormous chocolates.

'*Thank* you. More good luck. I don't know what's the matter with me this morning, but I keep on and on having good luck.'

'Well, you must have got something lucky on you,' said Twinkles, looking at him closely. 'Have you got a lucky feather in your hat? No. Have you got a lucky button on? No. Well *I* don't know what's making you lucky then. Did you pick a four-leaved clover today?'

'No,' said Toppy. 'I've never found one in my life, though I've always wanted to. I simply can't imagine why I'm lucky today.'

He went skipping on his way, and then felt the stone in his shoe again.

I really must take it out, he thought, and bent down to take off his shoe. And there on the ground, just under his nose, was a little pearl necklace!

'Look at that now!' said Toppy in amazement, forgetting all about taking off his shoe. 'A pearl necklace! Whatever next! I must take it along to the police station and see if anyone has lost it.'

Soon he was showing it to Mr Plod, the policeman.

'My word! Where did you find it?' said Mr Plod. 'It belongs to Lady Silver-Toes. There is a reward of five gold pieces offered to the finder. Here you are, Toppy. Go and spend them.'

'Well, would you believe it!' said Toppy in astonishment. 'Five gold pieces – all for picking up a necklace I saw under my nose! There's no end to my luck this morning!'

Off he went, eager to get back to his aunt and tell her all about this Good Luck Morning. She was in the garden, weeding. She waved to him as he came in. 'Toppy! I've left some hot ginger cakes on the table for you – and the postman has brought a parcel. It's from your grandmother, so it's sure to be something nice.'

'Well, well – what good luck is following me!' thought Toppy, pleased. He popped a ginger cake into his mouth, and cut the string round the parcel.

Out came a box, and in the box was just what Toppy had longed for for weeks. It was a magic top which, once it was set spinning, would go on without stopping, and would hum a little song all the time. Some of the pixies already had them and Toppy had longed and longed for one.

'Look! A magic top!' he cried, running out to his aunt.

'Lucky boy!' she said.

'But you wait till you hear all that has happened to me this morning,' said Toppy. 'Look, Aunt – look at all these gold pieces. I've had nothing but good luck all the morning.'

His aunt listened while he told her everything.

'It's most peculiar,' she said. 'There's *something* you've got on you somewhere, Toppy, that is bringing you this good luck. Whatever can it be?'

But Toppy couldn't think *what* it was. He looked up and down himself, but he was just the same as usual. It was most extraordinary.

'I'll just go and put these gold pieces into my moneybox,' he said, and he turned to go indoors. Then he felt the stone in his shoe again, and stopped.

'Bother! I've never taken that silly stone out – I've not had a minute to think about it! It's the only bit of bad luck I've had today.'

He took off his shoe. Inside was a sharp little stone, roughly in the shape of a star, and a very bright blue in colour. Toppy picked it out of his shoe and threw it high in the air. It fell in the road somewhere.

'What was that?' asked his aunt.

'A stone out of my shoe,' said Toppy, putting his shoe on again. 'It's been bothering me all morning. Now, Aunt, I'm going to look out for some more good luck!'

'Well, Toppy – I'm afraid you won't get it,' said his aunt. 'I know what has brought you all your good luck this morning – that little blue stone in your shoe! It was a good luck stone.'

Toppy stared at her in dismay. 'Was it? Are you sure? Oh my, oh my, I've thrown it away into the road. Goodness knows where it's gone. Oh, Aunt – I've thrown my good luck away!'

'What a thing to do!' said his aunt. 'Go and look for it before anyone else finds it, silly.'

But Toppy couldn't find that tiny stone though he spent hours looking in the road. Wasn't it a pity? It's somewhere about still, I expect, so if you get a stone in your shoe, do have a look at it before you shake it away. You might have a Good Luck Morning too, if you can get it!

Floppety Castle

Floppety Castle

'OH, DEAR,' SIGHED Donald, as he walked round his garden, 'I do wish Mummy would get better. She's been ill so long.'

'Tu-whit, tu-whit,' said a big white owl, sitting on a fence nearby. 'Why don't you get the magic Health Drink from Fairy Oriell.'

'Goodness, gracious,' said Donald, hardly believing his ears, 'that's the first time *I* ever heard an owl talk.'

'I'm Hoo, the White Owl of Fairyland,' said the big owl, blinking. 'I sometimes come to your world and see what's going on.'

'Can I *really* get a Health Drink from Fairyland?'

asked Donald excitedly. 'Tell me where to go, and I'll get it for Mummy.'

'Go down the lane, till you come to the big oak tree,' said Hoo. 'Knock three times and whistle once. Goodbye and good luck,' and he spread his big soft wings and flew away.

Donald ran down the lane till he came to the oak tree. He knocked three times and whistled.

'Come in. Come in,' shouted a voice, and Donald saw a little brown door slide sideways into the tree, leaving an entrance.

This is going to be an adventure, thought Donald, as he stepped inside and climbed up a winding staircase.

He came to a little room, and at one end sat a pixie reading a book.

'Good morning,' said Donald politely. 'Hoo said I was to come here, because I want to get the Health Drink for my mummy, who is ill.'

'Well, *I* haven't got it,' said the pixie. 'Oriell has it, and she's been taken a prisoner to Floppety Castle.'

'Oh, dear,' said Donald, disappointed. 'I *must* have it. Couldn't I go and rescue Oriell?'

'Certainly,' answered the pixie. 'But it won't be an easy job. Lots of fairies have tried and failed.'

'Oh, tell me where to go, and I'll start at once,' begged Donald.

'Well, go down to the Underground Caves,' said the pixie, 'then walk along till you come to the Gnome Railway. Get in and go to the Balloon Man's; he'll tell you what to do.'

'Thank you,' said Donald. 'I'll be sure to remember.'

'Here's the way to the Underground Caves,' said the pixie, opening a yellow trapdoor in the floor.

Donald saw a long flight of steps stretching down and down. He thought it all looked rather dark, but off he went, down hundreds of steps, lit by a dim yellow lamp here and there.

At last the steps stopped, and Donald found himself in a great blue cave.

Well, I'd better go through the caves till I come to the

Gnome Railway, thought Donald, running through the blue cave.

He passed into a small pink one, where slept a ring of magical brownies. Donald ran through without waking them, and came to a yellow cave full of happy dancing fairies, who all flew away as he entered.

On he went, through caves of all colours, until he came to one which had a pair of lines running through.

I'd better wait here till the Gnome Railway train comes along, thought Donald. Just as he spoke, a tiny engine came puffing along, dragging little carriages behind it. It stopped by Donald, and he got in. There were no seats, but big, soft cushions to sit on.

'Where are you going?' asked a big grey rabbit, making room for him.

'To the Balloon Man's,' answered Donald. 'Where do I get out?'

'At Breezy Corner,' answered the rabbit. 'It's the next station.'

On puffed the tiny train, out of the wonderful caves,

into the open air, through fields of lovely flowers and over tiny little bridges. At last it stopped again.

'Here you are!' said the grey rabbit. 'This is Breezy Corner.'

Donald jumped out and looked around. He saw a little crooked house in the distance, and in the front garden the Balloon Man was busy flying blue balloons. Donald ran over to him and went into the garden.

'Excuse me!' he cried. 'But the oak tree pixie said you might help me to find Oriell, who's a prisoner in Floppety Castle.'

'Well, you *are* brave!' said the Balloon Man. 'Oriell is guarded by hundreds of horrid little Red Elves. No one can get her free save by knocking the castle down, and no one has been brave enough to do *that* yet!'

'It sounds rather awful,' said Donald bravely, 'but I don't mind *anything*. You see, I want Oriell to give me the Health Drink for Mummy.'

'Well, do you see that hill over there?' asked the Balloon Man, pointing. 'That's Floppety Castle on the top. Take this hammer with you, you may find it useful.'

'Thank you,' said Donald. He made his way over the fields till he came to Floppety Castle. He walked boldly into the front door and looked around. It was a huge place, with pictures of kings and queens covering the walls.

'Go away, go away!' suddenly cried hundreds of voices, and Donald saw a crowd of little Red Elves rushing towards him, looking very fierce.

He swung his hammer.

'*You* go away!' he shouted bravely. 'I've come to rescue Oriell.'

'You can't! You can't! You've got to knock down the castle to do that!' jeered the little elves. 'And you'd get hurt if you did.'

'*I* don't mind!' cried Donald, and, raising his hammer, he crashed it against the castle wall.

Clitter-clatter, crash! Clitter-clatter, crash!

Down came the castle all in a heap, and the little Red Elves fled away, shrieking.

'Pooh!' said Donald. 'It's only a *card* castle! How silly!'

Sure enough it was! And there, coming towards him, Donald saw Fairy Oriell, a lovely, blue-winged fairy, holding out a bottle of golden liquid to him.

'Thank you, Donald,' she cried. 'You *are* brave to rescue me. I was under a spell till someone was bold enough to knock the castle down. I know what you want, so here is the magic Health Drink for your mummy.'

Donald took it, most delighted. Oriell waved her wand. A great wind rushed round Donald, and he gasped for breath and shut his eyes.

When he opened them again he was in his own garden.

'Mummy, Mummy!' he cried, running indoors with his precious little bottle. 'I've got the Health Drink for you!'

'You're a brave little boy, Donald,' said his mummy,

as she drank the magic drink, and heard all his adventures. 'Why, I believe I shall get better ever so quickly now!'

And of course she did, and the doctor *can't* think why!

The Wizard's Umbrella

The Wizard's Umbrella

RIBBY THE GNOME lived in a small cottage at the end of Tiptoe Village. Nobody liked him because he was always borrowing things and never bringing them back! It was most annoying of him.

The things he borrowed most were umbrellas. I really couldn't tell you how many umbrellas Ribby had borrowed in his life – hundreds, I should think! He had borrowed Dame Twinkle's nice red one, he had taken Mr Biscuit the Baker's old green one, he had had Pixie Dimple's little grey and pink sunshade, and many, many more.

If people came to ask for them back, he would hunt

all about and then say he was very sorry but he must have lent their umbrellas to someone else – he certainly hadn't got them in his cottage now. And no one would ever know what had happened to their nice umbrellas!

Of course, Ribby the gnome knew quite well where they were! They were all tied up tightly together hidden in his loft. And once a month, Ribby would set out on a dark night, when nobody was about, and take with him all the borrowed umbrellas. He would go to the town of Here-We-Are, a good many miles away, and then the next day he would go through the streets there, crying, 'Umbrellas for sale! Fine umbrellas!'

He would sell the whole bundle, and make quite a lot of money. Then the wicked gnome would buy himself some fine new clothes, and perhaps a new chair or some new curtains for his cottage, and go home again.

Now one day it happened that Dame Twinkle went over to the town of Here-We-Are, and paid a call on her cousin, Mother Tantrums. And there standing in the umbrella stand in Mother Tantrums' hall, Dame Twinkle saw her very own nice red umbrella, that she had lent to Ribby the gnome the month before!

She stared at it in great surprise. However did it come to be in her cousin's umbrella stand? Surely she hadn't lent it to Mother Tantrums? No, no – she was certain, quite certain, she had lent it to Ribby the gnome.

'What are you staring at?' asked Mother Tantrums in surprise.

'Well,' said Dame Twinkle, pointing to the red umbrella, 'it's a funny thing, Cousin Tantrums, but, you know, that's my red umbrella you've got in your umbrella stand.'

'Nonsense!' said Mother Tantrums. 'Why, that's an umbrella I bought for a shilling from a little gnome who often comes round selling things.'

'A *shilling*!' cried Dame Twinkle in horror. 'My goodness, gracious me, I paid sixteen shillings and ninepence for it! A shilling, indeed! What next!'

'What are you talking about?' asked Mother

Tantrums, quite cross. 'It's *my* umbrella, not yours – and a very good bargain it was too!'

'I should think so!' said Dame Twinkle, looking lovingly at the red umbrella, which she had been very fond of indeed. 'Tell me, Cousin, what sort of a gnome was this that sold you your umbrella?'

'Oh, he was short,' said Mother Tantrums.

'Lots of gnomes are short,' said Dame Twinkle. 'Can't you remember anything else about him?'

'Well, he wore a bright yellow scarf round his neck,' said Mother Tantrums, 'and his eyes were a very light green.'

'That's Ribby the gnome!' cried Dame Twinkle, quite certain. 'He always wears a yellow scarf, and his eyes are very green. Oh, the wicked scamp! I suppose he borrows our umbrellas in order to sell them when he can! Oh, the horrid little thief! I shall tell the wizard who lives in our village and ask him to punish Ribby. Yes, I will! He deserves a punishment indeed!'

So when she went back to Tiptoe Village, Dame

Twinkle went to call on the Wizard Deep-One. He was a great friend of hers, and when he heard about Ribby's wickedness he shook his head in horror.

'He must certainly be punished,' said the wizard, nodding his head. 'Leave it to me, Dame Twinkle. I will see to it.'

Deep-One thought for a long time, and then he smiled. Ha, he would lay a little trap for Ribby that would teach him never to borrow umbrellas again. He took a spell and with it he made a very fine umbrella indeed. It was deep blue, and for a handle it had a dog's head. It was really a marvellous umbrella.

The wizard put it into his umbrella stand and then left his front door open wide every day so that anyone passing by could see the dog's-head umbrella quite well. He was sure that Ribby the gnome would spy it the very first time he came walking by.

When Ribby did see the umbrella he stopped to have a good look at it. My, what a lovely umbrella! He hadn't noticed it before, so it must be a new one. See the dog's head on it, it looked almost real! Oh, if Ribby could only get *that* umbrella, he could sell it for a good many shillings in the town of Here-We-Are. He was sure that the enchanter who lived there would be very pleased to buy it.

Somehow or other I must get that umbrella, thought Ribby. *The very next time it rains I will hurry by the wizard's house, and pop in and ask him to lend it to me! I don't expect he will, but I'll ask, anyway!*

So on the Thursday following, when a rainstorm came, Ribby hurried out of his cottage without an umbrella and ran to Deep-One's house. The front door was wide open as usual and Ribby could quite well see the dog-headed umbrella in the umbrella stand. He ran up the path, and knocked at the open door.

'Who's there?' came the wizard's voice.

'It's me, Ribby the gnome!' said the gnome. 'Please, Wizard Deep-One, could you lend me an umbrella? It's pouring with rain and I am getting so wet. I am sure I shall get a dreadful cold if someone doesn't lend me an umbrella.'

'Dear, dear, dear!' said the wizard, coming out of his parlour, and looking at the wet gnome. 'You certainly are *very* wet! Yes, I will lend you an umbrella – but mind, Ribby, let me warn you to bring it back tomorrow in case something unpleasant happens to you.'

'Oh, of course, of course,' said Ribby. 'I always return things I borrow, wizard. You shall have it back tomorrow as sure as eggs are eggs.'

'Well, take that one from the umbrella stand, Ribby,' said the wizard, pointing to the dog's-head umbrella. Ribby took it in delight. He had got what he wanted. How easy it had been after all! Ho, ho, he wouldn't bring it back tomorrow, not he! He would take it to the town of Here-We-Are as soon as ever he could and sell it to the enchanter there. What luck!

He opened it, said thank you to the smiling wizard, and rushed down the path with the blue umbrella. He was half afraid the wizard would call him back – but no, Deep-One let him go without a word – but he chuckled very deeply as he saw the gnome vanishing round the corner. How easily Ribby had fallen into the trap!

Of course Ribby didn't take the umbrella back the next day. No, he put it up in his loft and didn't go near the wizard's house at all. If he saw the wizard in the street he would pop into a shop until he had gone by. He wasn't going to let him have his umbrella back for a moment!

Now after three weeks had gone by, and Ribby had heard nothing from the wizard about his umbrella, he decided it would be safe to go to Here-We-Are and sell it.

I expect the wizard has forgotten all about it by now, thought Ribby. *He is very forgetful.*

So that night Ribby packed up three other umbrellas, and tied the wizard's dog-headed one to them very carefully. Then he put the bundle over his shoulder and set out in the darkness. Before morning came he was in the town of Here-We-Are, and the folk there heard him crying out his wares in a loud voice.

'Umbrellas for sale! Fine umbrellas for sale! Come and buy!'

Ribby easily sold the other three umbrellas he had with him and then he made his way to the enchanter's house. The dog-headed umbrella was now the only one left.

The enchanter came to the door and looked at the umbrella that Ribby showed him. But, as soon as his eye fell on it, he drew back in horror.

'Buy that umbrella!' he cried. 'Not I! Why, it's alive!'

'Alive!' said Ribby, laughing scornfully. 'No, sir, it is as dead as a doornail!'

'I tell you, that umbrella is *alive*!' said the enchanter and he slammed the door in the astonished gnome's face.

Ribby looked at the dog-headed umbrella, feeling very much puzzled – and as he looked, a very peculiar feeling came over him. The dog's head really did look alive. It wagged one ear as Ribby looked at it, and then it showed its teeth at the gnome and growled fiercely!

My goodness! Ribby was frightened almost out of his life! He dropped the umbrella on to the ground and fled away as fast as his little legs would carry him!

As soon as the umbrella touched the ground, a very peculiar thing happened to it. It grew four legs, and the head became bigger. The body was made of the long umbrella part, and the tail was the end bit. It could even wag!

'Oh, oh, an umbrella-dog!' cried all the people of Here-We-Are town and they fled away in fright. But the strange dog took no notice of anyone but Ribby the gnome. He galloped after him, barking loudly.

His umbrella-body flapped as he went along on his stout little doggy legs, and his tongue hung out of his mouth. It was most astonishing. People looked out of their windows at it, and everyone closed their front doors with a bang in case the strange umbrella-dog should come running into their houses.

Ribby was dreadfully frightened. He ran on and on, and every now and then he looked round.

'Oh, my goodness, that umbrella-dog's still after me!' he panted. 'What shall I do? Oh, why, why, why did I borrow the wizard's umbrella? Why didn't I take it back? I might have known there would be something strange about it!'

The umbrella-dog raced on, and came so near to Ribby that it was able to snap at his twinkling legs. Snap! The dog's teeth took a piece out of Ribby's green trousers!

'Ow! Ooh! Ow!' shrieked Ribby in horror, and he shot on twice as fast, panting like a railway train going up a hill! Everybody watched from their windows and some of them laughed because it was really a very peculiar sight.

Ribby looked out for someone to open a door so that he could run in. But every single door was shut. He must just run on and on. But how much longer could he run? He was getting terribly out of breath.

The umbrella-dog was enjoying himself very much.

Ho, this was better fun than being a dull old umbrella! This was seeing life! If only he could catch that running thing in front, what fun he would have!

The umbrella-dog ran a bit faster and caught up to Ribby once more. This time he jumped up and bit a piece out of the gnome's lovely yellow scarf.

'OW!' yelled Ribby, jumping high into the air. 'OW! You horrid cruel dog! Leave me alone! How dare you, I say?'

The dog sat down to chew the piece he had bitten out of Ribby's yellow scarf, and the gnome ran on, hoping that the dog would forget about him.

'Oh, if only I could get home!' cried the panting gnome. 'Once I'm in my house I'm safe!'

He ran on and on, through the wood and over the common that lay between the town of Here-We-Are and the village of Tiptoe. The dog did not seem to be following him. Ribby kept looking round but there was no umbrella-dog there. If only he could get home in time!

Just as he got to Tiptoe Village he heard a pattering of feet behind him. He looked round and saw the umbrella-dog just behind him. Oh, what a shock for poor Ribby!

'Look, look!' cried everyone in surprise. 'There's an angry umbrella-dog after Ribby. Run, Ribby, run!'

Poor Ribby had to run all through the village of Tiptoe to get to his cottage. The dog ran at his heels snapping every now and again, making the gnome leap high into the air with fright.

'I'll never, never, never borrow an umbrella again, or anything else!' vowed the gnome. 'Oh, why didn't I take the wizard's umbrella back?'

At last he was home. He rushed up the path, pushed the door open and slammed it. But, alas, the umbrella-dog had slipped in with him, and there it was in front of Ribby, sitting up and begging.

'OH, you horror!' shouted Ribby, trying to open the door and get out again. But the dog wouldn't let him. Every time Ribby put his hand on the handle of the door it jumped up at him. So at last he stopped trying to open it and looked in despair at the strange dog, who was now sitting up and begging.

'Do you want something to eat?' said the gnome. 'Goodness, I shouldn't have thought an umbrella-dog could be hungry. Wait a bit. I've a nice joint of meat here, you shall have that, if only you will stop snapping at me!'

The dog ran by Ribby as he went hurriedly to his larder and opened the door. He took a joint of meat from a dish and gave it to the dog, which crunched it up hungrily.

Then began a very sorrowful time for Ribby! The dog wouldn't leave him for a moment and the gnome had never in his life known such a hungry creature. Although its body was simply an umbrella, it ate and ate and ate. Ribby spent all his money on food for it. The dog wouldn't leave his side, and when the gnome went out shopping the strange creature always went with him, much to the surprise and amusement of all the people in the village.

'Look!' they would cry. 'Look! There goes Ribby the gnome and his umbrella-dog! Where did he get it from? Why does he keep such a strange, hungry creature?'

If Ribby tried to creep off at night, or run away from the dog, it would at once start snapping and snarling at his heels, and after it had bitten a large hole in his best coat, Ribby gave up trying to go away.

'But what shall I do?' wondered the little gnome, each night, as he looked at his empty larder. 'This dog is eating everything I have. I shall soon have no money left to buy anything.'

Ribby had had such a shock when the stolen umbrella had turned into the umbrella-dog, that he had never once thought of borrowing anything else. He felt much too much afraid that what he borrowed would turn into something like the dog, and he really couldn't bear that!

'I suppose I'd better get some work to do,' he said to himself at last. 'But who will give me a job? Nobody likes me because I have always borrowed things and never taken them back. Oh, dear, how foolish and silly I have been.'

Then at last he thought he had better go to the Wizard Deep-One and confess to him all that had happened. Perhaps Deep-One would take away the horrid umbrella-dog and then Ribby would feel happier. So off he went to the wizard's house.

The wizard opened the door himself and when he saw Ribby with the dog he began to laugh. How he laughed! He held his sides and roared till the tears ran down his cheeks.

'What's the matter?' asked Ribby in surprise. 'What is the joke?'

'*You* are!' cried the wizard, laughing more than ever. 'Ho, ho, Ribby, little did you think that I had made that dog-headed umbrella especially for you to borrow and that I knew exactly what was going to happen! Well, you can't say that I didn't warn you. My only surprise is that you haven't come to me before for help. You can't have liked having such a strange umbrella-dog living with you, eating all your food, and snapping at your heels every moment! But it's a good punishment for you – you won't borrow things and not bring them back again, I'm sure!'

'I never, never will,' said Ribby, going very red. 'I am very sorry for all the wrong things I have done. Perhaps I had better keep this umbrella-dog to remind me to be honest, wizard.'

'No, I'll have it,' said Deep-One. 'It will do to guard my house for me. I think any burglar would run for miles if he suddenly saw the umbrella-dog coming for him. And what are *you* going to do, Ribby? Have you any work?'

'No,' said Ribby sorrowfully. 'Nobody likes me and I'm sure no one will give me any work to do in case I borrow something and don't return it, just as I used to do.'

'Well, well, well,' said the wizard, and his wrinkled eyes looked kindly at the sad little gnome. 'You have learnt your lesson, Ribby, I can see. Come and be my gardener and grow my vegetables. I shall work you hard, but I shall pay you well, and I think you will be happy.'

So Ribby is now Deep-One's gardener, and he works hard from morning to night. But he is happy because everyone likes him now – and as for the umbrella-dog, he is as fond of Ribby as anyone else is and keeps at his heels all the time. And the funny thing is that Ribby likes him there!

My Goodness, What a Joke!

My Goodness, What a Joke!

ONE DAY MRS Well-I-Never came rushing to speak to her brother, Grabbit the gnome.

'Grabbit!' she said. 'Where are you? I've got news for you! Look what I've found.'

'What?' asked Grabbit disagreeably. 'You always find such silly things, stones with holes in, or four-leaved clovers that aren't lucky, or things that belong to someone else!'

'Well, you just see what I've got!' said Mrs Well-I-Never, and she opened her hand and showed something to Grabbit. It was a tiny box of blue powder.

'It's a blue spell!' said Mrs Well-I-Never. 'Dame

Dandy must have dropped it on her way up the hill this morning. It's the same kind of spell that she put in her cauldron on the day you fell into it and came out blue. Don't you remember?'

'I'm hardly likely to forget while my nose is still blue,' said Grabbit gloomily. 'Throw the spell away, Sister, I don't like blue spells.'

'No, but listen,' said Mrs Well-I-Never. 'You know we've always wanted to pay little Shuffle back for making you fall into Dame Dandy's blue spell? Well, now we've got a wonderful way to get even with him.'

'How?' said surly Grabbit.

'Do listen, Grabbit,' said Mrs Well-I-Never. 'I'll make a cake, and I'll put this blue spell into it, and I'll send it along to Ma Shuffle because it is her birthday! She'll eat it and so will Shuffle, and they'll both turn blue!'

'Ha ha, ho ho!' roared Grabbit suddenly. 'That's a good joke. Oh, that's the best joke I ever heard. Make your cake, quickly!'

So Mrs Well-I-Never made the cake. It was a

beauty, crammed with fruit. She shook the blue powder into it and baked it. 'It's a pity I can't ice it,' she said. 'I haven't any icing sugar.'

'Oh, never mind about that,' said Grabbit. 'Is it ready? Well, take it down to Ma Shuffle at once. Ho, ho, what will she and little Shuffle look like tomorrow? Oh, what a joke this is, what a joke!'

'Well, I never! I've not seen you so pleased for years!' said his sister. 'Well, I'll go now. And don't you give our secret away to anyone!'

Ma Shuffle was surprised and pleased with Mrs Well-I-Never's present of a cake. 'Thank you,' she said. 'Do come to my party this afternoon and share the cake, will you?'

'Oh, no, thank you,' said Mrs Well-I-Never at once. 'That would never do! Well, happy birthday, Ma!'

'Look at that,' said Ma to little Shuffle. 'There's kindness even in Mrs Well-I-Never. What a pity she sent me a cake though – I've such an enormous one already, and it's iced so beautifully.'

'Ma, send Mrs Well-I-Never's cake to Mrs Nearby,' said Shuffle. 'We've got enough cake, really, and it's nice to be generous if we can. Mrs Nearby can't come to your party, she's not well. She'd love a cake for herself!'

'Bless your kind heart, little Shuffle,' said Ma. 'You take it along then, with my best wishes.'

So the blue spell cake was taken over to Mrs Nearby's by little Shuffle. Mrs Nearby was in bed and couldn't come to the door, so Shuffle pushed the cake in through the window.

'Thank you, little Shuffle, you're kind,' said Mrs Nearby. 'I'm expecting the doctor soon, and maybe he'll tell me I can get up.'

The doctor did come, very soon after that. He was Doctor Healem, and he was just like his name. He shook his head over Mrs Nearby.

'No, you can't get up yet,' he said. 'And what's this rich fruit cake I see here on the windowsill? You mustn't eat anything like that yet, Mrs Nearby.'

'Oh, dear, well, will you take it away and give it to someone?' said Mrs Nearby. 'I might nibble a bit if you don't, it looks so good.'

'Yes, I'll take it to Mrs Shifty,' said Doctor Healem, and he took it away with him. But Mrs Shifty was out, so he left the cake just by the front door. She found it there when she came home.

'Look at that! Somebody has left a cake here for me!' she said. 'Well, I'd keep it, only I'm going away tomorrow and it would get stale in my larder. I'd better give it away.'

So what did she do but take it that very afternoon to Mrs Button. Mrs Button was pleased.

'Well, that's nice of you,' she said. 'I'll let little Button have it for his tea. I don't like fruit cake myself, so he can eat it all. He'll start off with five or six slices, I expect!'

But little Button was very naughty that afternoon. 'Now you just shan't have that beautiful cake!' scolded Mrs Button. 'I'm ashamed of you, spoiling your nice new coat like that! Don't you know wet paint when you see it? Don't you—'

'All right, Ma, all right,' said Button. 'I won't have the cake. Don't go on and on at me though! What shall I do with the cake?'

'You take it to Mrs Popalong,' said Ma Button. 'Go along now – and don't you go near that wet paint on the way!'

Button went to Mrs Popalong's. She was very busy baking. 'Mrs Popalong, I've brought you something from Ma!' called Button.

'Put it down on the hall table,' called back Mrs Popalong. 'I'm busy this morning, little Button. You put it there and I'll see to it when I've finished.'

So Button left the cake on the hall table, and when Mrs Popalong came along to see what he had left, she laughed aloud.

'Well, I would get a present of a cake just when it's my baking day and I've made six!' she said. 'It's a nice enough cake too – but it looks a bit battered somehow, round the top. I'll ice it when I ice mine and send it off to someone else. I know Pa Popalong won't eat any cakes but mine, so it's no good keeping this one!'

Well, she iced it beautifully in pink and white and put pink roses on top. Now, who should she send it to? Everyone was going to Ma Shuffle's party this afternoon – but wait! Didn't she hear Ma say that Mrs Well-I-Never and Grabbit weren't going? Well, she'd send them the cake then! They'd be glad of it, if they were missing the party.

So kind Mrs Popalong walked to Mrs Well-I-Never's house and offered her the iced cake. Mrs Well-I-Never was thrilled to see it.

'Well, I never!' she said. 'I never did see such a fine cake. Did you ice it yourself, Mrs Popalong?'

'Yes,' said Mrs Popalong. 'But I didn't make the cake. I don't know who made it – little Button brought it along this morning. Well, I hope you enjoy it, Mrs Well-I-Never!'

'Grabbit!' called Mrs Well-I-Never that teatime.

'Come and have tea. Mrs Popalong's sent a fine iced cake for us!'

'Oh, good!' said Grabbit, and he sat down at the table. 'My, it certainly is a fine-looking cake. I say, Sister, do you suppose little Shuffle and his ma are sitting down gobbling up that blue spell cake?'

'Yes!' said Mrs Well-I-Never. 'Oh, what a joke! I'm glad I'm not having a bit!'

'I'm glad too,' said Grabbit, taking his second slice of cake. 'It's the best joke I ever heard in my life. Ha ha, ho ho ho! What a joke!'

Well, it was, of course – but not quite in the way they meant. By the end of teatime they were both as blue as cornflowers!

My goodness, what a joke!

The Fairy and the Policeman

The Fairy and the Policeman

ONE NIGHT A fairy wandered into the nursery, where the toys were all talking and playing together. They were delighted to see her, and begged her to tell them all about herself.

'Well, I live under the white lilac bush in the garden,' she said. 'But, you know, I'm afraid I shall soon have to move.'

'Why?' asked the toys in surprise.

'Because,' said the fairy with a shiver, 'a great frog has come to live there. I don't mind frogs a bit usually, but this one *is* so cold and clammy! I am so afraid that he will bring his brothers and sisters there too.'

'Dear me,' said the toy policeman, in a shocked voice. 'But, you know, dear fairy, frogs have no right to go to the place you have made your home. That is trespassing, and isn't allowed.'

'Well, how can I prevent them?' said the fairy. 'They are much stronger than I am.'

'Look,' said the toy policeman, taking a whistle from his pocket. 'Here is a police whistle. Take it home with you to the lilac bush. If those frogs do come, blow it loudly and I will come to your help.'

'Oh, thank you,' said the fairy, and she slipped the whistle into her pocket. Off she went, out of the window, waving merrily to the toys.

And the very next night, just as the toys were playing 'Here we go round the Mulberry Bush', they heard the police whistle being blown very loudly indeed.

'The fairy is whistling for help!' cried the policeman, and he jumped out of the window. He ran to the white lilac bush, and underneath he saw such a strange sight.

There were seven yellow and green frogs, all

crowding round the poor fairy, and she was frightened. The policeman drew his truncheon, and began to push away the frogs. They squeaked and croaked and began to hop away.

'Come back to the nursery with me,' begged the toy policeman. 'You'll be safe there. I'm afraid the frogs might come back again when you are asleep.'

So the fairy went back to the nursery with the policeman, and all the toys welcomed her. She played games with them and had a perfectly lovely time. When they were hungry they went to the little toy sweetshop and bought some peppermint rock. It was great fun!

'I do wish I could live here with you,' said the fairy. 'It's so jolly.'

'Well, why can't you?' asked the policeman. 'There's plenty of room in the toy cupboard. We can hide you right at the back.'

So that night the fairy slept in the toy cupboard with all the other toys – and what do you think? Early the next morning, Gwen, the little girl who lived in the nursery, went to the cupboard and began to pull all the toys out. Oh, how the fairy trembled!

'Keep quite still and pretend you are a toy doll,' whispered the policeman. So she did.

'Oh, oh! Here's a beautiful fairy doll!' cried Gwen, suddenly seeing the fairy. 'Where did she come from? Oh, Mummy, look!'

She pulled out the doll and showed it to her mother. The fairy kept so still and made herself so stiff that she really did look just like a fairy doll.

'Isn't she beautiful?' cried the little girl. 'Where did she come from, Mummy?'

'Well, really, I don't know,' said Mummy, surprised. 'I've never seen her before. It's the nicest toy you have, Gwen.'

Gwen played with the fairy doll all day long and loved her very much. The fairy was delighted, and when night came and all the toys came alive once more, she danced round the nursery in joy.

'I shall be a toy now instead of a fairy,' she cried. 'I shall live with you in the cupboard and be happy.'

'Hurrah!' shouted the toys. 'What fun!'

The fairy is still there, and Gwen is very fond of her. Wouldn't she be surprised if she knew that her doll is really a fairy?

Who Came Creeping in the Door?

Who Came Creeping in the Door?

HOBBLE LIVED IN a tiny cottage all by himself. He was very fond of ginger biscuits and big round peppermints, and he kept a tin of each on his mantelpiece.

He made the biscuits every Tuesday and the peppermints every Saturday, and when his old aunt came to see him on Wednesday and Sunday there were always plenty to offer her.

And then one day Hobble was puzzled. It was a Wednesday and his aunt came to see him. He took the tin down from his mantelpiece and opened it. His aunt looked inside.

'Dear me, Hobble,' she said. 'You've only got two biscuits left! Didn't you bake them yesterday as usual?'

'Yes, I certainly did,' said Hobble. 'I made a whole tinful. What a peculiar thing!'

And then on Sunday when his aunt came, and he took down his peppermint tin, what a surprise! There were hardly any peppermints there, although he had nearly filled the tin on Saturday!

'Somebody comes creeping in at your door when you go out shopping,' said his aunt. 'Yes, somebody comes in and takes your ginger biscuits and your peppermints, Hobble, no doubt about that!'

'Oh, dear!' said Hobble. 'How very horrid! Who can it be? The children all come by my cottage on their way to and from school. I suppose it must be one of them. But the little thief will never own up.'

'Of course he won't,' said his aunt. 'You must find out yourself.'

'But how?' asked Hobble.

'I'll tell you,' said his aunt, and she whispered into his ear. He nodded his head.

'Yes, yes, I'll do that! A very good idea of yours, Aunt. I'd rather not do the spying myself. I'll set all those things to do the work for me instead.'

Well, the next day, before he went out shopping, Hobble set a few things about the room. He took a pincushion and in it he put six needles with big eyes. He went out and picked six stalks of corn and put them in a vase on his mantelpiece. Their ears rustled together prettily.

And then he put three pairs of shoes on the floor below the mantelpiece, with their six tongues sticking out well.

'There!' said Hobble. 'Now do your work, all of you!'

He went out to do his shopping. There were no biscuits or sweets taken from the tin that day, nor the next. But on the next day the tins were almost empty.

'Who is it that comes creeping through my door?'

wondered Hobble. 'It must be one of the children. What a pity!'

Now, the next day Hobble asked all the schoolchildren to come and see him. 'I want to show you a bit of magic,' he told them. 'So come along.'

The children were pleased. They thought Hobble was a very good conjurer, and they came crowding in after school.

'Now, children,' said Hobble, 'I want to ask you something. Someone has been creeping in at my door, and has been taking my ginger biscuits and my peppermints. I don't know who it is. Before I find out by magic, I want to ask you if you know who it is? Will the thief please be brave and own up? Then I will forgive him, and he shall promise me never to do such a bad thing again.'

But nobody owned up. The top boy of the class, Billy Bold, spoke quite rudely to Hobble.

'Who wants your old biscuits and sweets? We get enough money to buy all we want!'

He was a big boy, strong and handsome. He was a clever boy too, and all the children looked up to him.

'Yes,' they said, anxious to say the same as the great Billy Bold, 'yes, we get enough money of our own to buy biscuits and sweets without bothering about *yours*, Hobble!'

Hobble looked rather sad. 'Well, I shall have to do a bit of magic then, to find out what I want to know,' he said. 'Now, listen, children. I have done no spying myself, but others have watched for me. See, these are the watchers!'

He pointed to the pincushion with its six needles, to the six stalks of corn in their vase, and to the three pairs of shoes below. The children stared in wonder, and Billy Bold and one or two others laughed scornfully.

'He's strange,' said one of them, behind his hand. Hobble heard.

'No,' he said, 'I'm not strange. You will soon see how clever I am, not mad!'

He threaded the six needles with white thread and then stuck them into a piece of black cloth.

'Whom did you see, with your six little eyes?' said Hobble in a loud voice to the needles. 'Tell me his name, needles!'

And, before the children's astonished eyes, the six needles began to sew all by themselves. Stitch after stitch they made in the black cloth, and the white threads showed up clearly.

'Billy Bold!' they wrote in big white stitches. 'Billy Bold!'

'Billy Bold!' said all the children in low, shocked voices. 'Is he the thief?'

'It's not true,' said Billy Bold loudly. 'All a silly trick. How dare you, Hobble?'

The six needles had now used up all their thread, and they stopped sewing. Hobble took down the vase of cornstalks. Their dry ears rattled together. He set them on the table near the children, and bent over them.

'Whom did you hear, with your six ears, golden corn?' asked Hobble. 'Whisper me his name!'

Then, as if they were blown by the breeze, the six ears of corn began rustling together and whispering. 'It was-s-s-s Billy Bold! It was-s-s-ssss Billy Bold! Ss-ss-ss!'

The children could hear what the corn whispered quite plainly. They looked scared. Billy Bold went rather pale. But he was still very defiant.

'Pooh! Another trick! What nonsense!'

'And now we will see what my shoes say,' said Hobble. 'They have tongues to speak with. Shoes, who comes creeping in at my door when I am gone?'

All the six tongues flapped and spoke at once. 'Billy Bold! Billy Bold! Billy Bold!'

Then Billy Bold sank down suddenly into a chair, his face very white. 'It's strange,' he said. 'It must be magic after all. I don't understand it.'

All the children looked at him. '*Was* it you, Billy

Bold, who took the biscuits and the sweets?' asked a boy.

'It was, it was, it was!' shouted all the shoe-tongues, and the ears of corn whispered again.

Billy Bold hung his head. 'Yes, I took them,' he said. 'I'm so ashamed. Now you all know me for what I am! Hobble, I'm sorry.'

'Are you?' said Hobble in a mild sort of voice. 'Well, people who are sorry for doing wrong usually do something to show they are.'

'Yes, they do,' said the children. 'Billy, what are you going to do?'

'I don't know. But I'll do *something*,' said Billy, his face now a bright red. 'Please, all of you, don't tell my mother. She'd be so upset.'

'We won't tell anybody, if you really *are* sorry,' said Hobble. 'It shall be a secret.'

Well, Billy Bold kept his word and tried to show that he really was sorry. He came and weeded Hobble's garden for him. He cleaned out his hens twice a week.

And he mended his gate for him so that it would open and shut properly.

Sometimes Hobble offers him a biscuit or a sweet, but Billy always shakes his head. 'I can't bear the taste of ginger or peppermint now,' he says. 'Thank you all the same, sir!'

It was a strange way to find the name of the thief who came creeping in at the door, wasn't it? I'd like to have heard those shoe-tongues shouting. It *would* have given me a surprise!

Roundy and the Keys

Roundy and the Keys

ONCE UPON A time there lived a gnome called Roundy. He had the jolliest little full-moon of a face you ever saw!

He was a locksmith, and made all kinds of keys. He lived just on the outside of Fairyland in a little round house built at the edge of a wood. The reason why he lived *outside* Fairyland instead of inside was because so many fairies lost their keys in our world and found they couldn't open the doors that led back into Fairyland. So they used to fly off to Roundy's cottage and buy new keys.

'I shouldn't get nearly so much trade if I didn't

live outside Fairyland!' chuckled Roundy, as he handed over a key to the sixteenth fairy one day.

* * * *

Now, of course, Roundy only sold keys to fairies, elves, magical brownies and their like. He knew quite well no one else was allowed in Fairyland unless they were taken there by the fairies themselves.

But one day a little girl came along that way. She was following a pixie, and was greatly excited. The pixie had no idea anyone was following, and danced along merrily.

'I've lost my key,
I've lost my key,
It's just like me!
Oh, just like me!
I'm on my way to Roundy Gnome
To buy a key to take me home!'

So sang the pixie at the top of his silvery little voice. The little girl followed, keeping herself hidden as much as she could, for she was terribly afraid the pixie would disappear if he saw her.

At last he came to Roundy's fat little house. He hopped in, while the little girl waited behind a tree. Then he hopped out again, carrying an odd-shaped key, rather like the sort with which we wind up clocks.

'I've got my key,
And now to see
If it will fit the door.
In Fairyland
Quite soon I'll stand,
And see my friends once more!'

The singing pixie ran up to a big beech tree and put his key into a keyhole in the trunk.

Creak, creak! A little door swung open, the pixie popped inside, shut the door, and disappeared!

* * * *

The little girl watched breathlessly. Then she ran up to the beech tree and tried her hardest to open the door she saw there.

Alas! It was locked.

'If only I had a key!' said the little girl. 'I could get into Fairyland and see all sorts of lovely things! I really, really could!'

She turned and looked at Roundy's cottage. In the window was a notice.

KEYS FOR FAIRYLAND
SOLD HERE.

'I'll buy one!' said the little girl. 'I've got a penny in my pocket, and that will surely be enough to pay!'

She ran into the cottage. It was the strangest little

place. Keys of all kinds and sizes hung round the walls, and in the middle of the tiny room sat Roundy hard at work making another key.

'Hallo, hallo!' he said in surprise. 'Where did you come from, little girl?'

'I've come to buy a key for Fairyland, please,' said she, putting down her penny on the table.

'I'm sorry to disappoint you,' said Roundy, 'but I can only sell keys to fairies!'

'*Please!*' said the little girl. 'I love fairies, and I only just want to peep in and then come out.'

'No,' said Roundy firmly. 'Run away, now.'

She didn't run away, she began to cry.

'I th-th-thought you'd be nice,' she said. 'You've g-g-got such a kind face, and n-now you're b-b-being horrid!'

'Bless my boots!' said Roundy. 'For goodness' sake don't cry. I can't bear it. Dry your eyes, my dear, dry your eyes!'

'Boo-hoo!' wept the little girl. 'BOO-HOO!'

Roundy was terribly upset. He was very kind-hearted, and he didn't know *what* to do. Suddenly he took down a key and pushed it into the little girl's hand.

'Here you are!' he said. 'That's what you want, isn't it? Take back your penny and run away now. But for goodness' sake don't tell anyone that you got a key here, will you?'

The little girl promised, dried her eyes, and ran off. She unlocked the door in the beech tree and went down the steps into Fairyland.

* * * *

It was lovely. She saw hundreds of fairies, magical brownies, elves and gnomes, and nobody took any notice of her at all. They thought she had been brought there by one of the fairies.

'I *must* go back and fetch Tim and Tony!' said the little girl. 'They'll be *so* surprised!'

So the next day she took Tim and Tony, her brothers,

down to Fairyland. They were tremendously astonished, for they hadn't believed in Fairyland before.

'Let's take Nurse!' they said. So the next day after that Nurse went down too – and she really could hardly believe her eyes!

When she got back home she told her master and mistress about the marvellous things she had seen – and *they* went and had a peep into Fairyland as well!

'Dear, dear me!' said the father when he arrived home again. 'Dear, dear me! What a most extraordinary thing! Can't we make up a party of people and take them all for an excursion to Fairyland? It really would be most original!'

No sooner said than done. A party of twenty grown-ups arrived in motorcars near the beech tree. The father had the key to the little door and opened it. In went everyone, all except one man, who was just a little too tall. To his great disappointment he had to stay outside alone – but not for long.

For in two minutes back came everyone in a most

tremendous hurry, tumbling out of the little door as fast as ever they could.

'Bless my buttons!' exclaimed the tall man who had been left outside. 'What's the matter?'

'Oh, hundreds and hundreds of fairies chased us,' panted the father. 'They threatened to turn us all into black beetles if we didn't get out quickly. They said we'd no right to be there without their permission!'

'Well, I suppose you hadn't,' said the tall man. 'Never mind, we'll go again later on.'

'We can't,' said the father. 'I dropped my key down there. I know! We'll ask my little girl to tell us where she got it, and we can easily get another one. This discovery is too great to give up lightly!'

But the little girl wouldn't tell them where she got the key.

'I can't,' she said, 'because I promised not to.'

All this time there was a great disturbance in Fairyland.

'How could those people have come here?' demanded the queen.

'I've found a key they dropped!' called an elf, holding it up. 'It's one of Roundy's, so they must have got it from him, and then found the little door!'

'How *dare* Roundy sell one of our keys to mortals!' cried the queen, who really was most upset and worried. 'I shall go straight to him and find out what he has done.'

* * * *

So off she flew, and descended angrily on Roundy.

'Have you sold a key to any mortal?' she asked the surprised little gnome.

'Er-no, not *sold* one,' said Roundy nervously. 'I – er – *gave* one to a little girl, Your Majesty. She wouldn't stop crying till I did!'

The queen frowned and told him what a dreadful result his carelessness had had.

'We might have had the whole of Fairyland discovered and taken by these interfering mortals!' she cried. 'All through your foolish kind-heartedness! You'd better come and live in Fairyland, Roundy, I can't trust you outside!'

'But what will fairies do if they lose their keys and can't buy others here?' asked Roundy.

'Oh, we'll manage that all right,' said the queen. 'We'll choose a certain kind of tree and hang hundreds of keys on it. Among them shall be one or two Fairyland keys that only *we* shall recognise. Then all that fairies will have to do is just go to the tree, pick off a magic key, fit it in the nearest fairy-door, and there you are!'

So it was decided. And now Roundy lives in Fairyland and doesn't do nearly such a big trade – but he is quite happy.

As for the tree the queen chose, you're sure to know it. It's the sycamore, of course. It's full of hanging keys now – but dear me, it's very difficult to know which are the one or two fairy keys. People *do* say that the proper ones have a tiny R for Roundy on them – but even if you find one you've still got to find the door!

So you see, Fairyland is well protected now.

Mr Pink-Whistle is a Conjurer!

Mr Pink-Whistle is a Conjurer!

MR PINK-WHISTLE WAS going along the road one morning, when he saw a notice tied neatly to a garden gate. He stopped to read it.

A CONJURING SHOW, FULL OF MAGIC AND MARVEL, WILL BE GIVEN IN OUR GARAGE TOMORROW AFTERNOON, AT THREE O'CLOCK. TICKETS: CHILDREN 3 SHILLINGS GROWN-UPS 6 SHILLINGS. THE MONEY IS TO GO TO OLD MRS JORDAN, TO BUY HER A WHEELCHAIR.

'Well, well – I think I'd better attend this conjuring

show,' said Mr Pink-Whistle. 'I know old Mrs Jordan. She used to keep the sweetshop, and always gave the children a few extra sweets in their bags! Then she broke her leg and couldn't walk, and now people are helping to buy her a wheelchair. Yes – I must certainly go!'

A boy came running to the gate when he saw Mr Pink-Whistle there. 'Are you reading my notice?' he said. 'Oh, I hope you are coming, sir – we want the garage absolutely full. You see, we want to buy—'

'Yes, I've read all about it,' said Pink-Whistle. 'I'm very pleased to help. I've known old Mrs Jordan for years. May I ask who the conjurer is going to be?'

'Well – actually I'm doing the conjuring,' said the boy. 'My name's Derek Fuller, and I had a marvellous conjuring set for Christmas. I've practised and practised, and I know quite a lot of tricks now. Come and see my conjuring set. It's in the garage.'

Mr Pink-Whistle went into the garage and saw the conjuring set. 'I can make an egg come in an empty bag,' said Derek. 'And five ribbons out of one ribbon. And I can put four hankies on top of one another, shake them out – and they'll all suddenly be tied together – and . . .'

'You are certainly clever,' said Pink-Whistle admiringly. 'I shall look forward to tomorrow. May I buy six tickets, please, as I would like to bring a few friends. And how much would you charge for a cat to come?'

'A cat! Well, I hadn't really thought,' said Derek, surprised. 'What about one penny?'

'Well – say tuppence,' said Pink-Whistle. 'It's my pet cat I want to bring – he does so enjoy things of this kind. Let me see now – that's one pound sixteen shillings and tuppence. Here you are.'

'Oh, thank you,' said Derek, and gave him the tickets, made of neatly cut-out bits of paper. 'That's the one for the cat – I've marked 2d on it. Three o'clock tomorrow, sir. See you then!'

But Mr Pink-Whistle saw Derek before three

o'clock the next day – he saw him when he came back from his walk half an hour later, looking very miserable indeed. He was taking down the notice from the gate. 'Hey – what's happened?' said Pink-Whistle in astonishment. 'Is the conjuring show off?'

'Yes, and I'll have to give you your money back,' said Derek. 'You remember when I took you into the garage to show you my conjuring set? Well, I must have left the doors open and someone came in after I'd gone, and stole my conjuring set! I do feel so terribly upset about it.'

'What a very mean trick!' said Pink-Whistle, shocked. 'Who was it? Have you any idea?'

'Yes. Tom, the big boy down the street,' said Derek. 'He's always wanted to borrow my set and I wouldn't lend it to him, because I knew I'd never get it back. I saw him running down the road a few minutes ago with a big red box under his arm – I'm sure he took it.'

'Well, never mind. We'll still have the conjuring show. I'm a bit of a conjurer myself you know,' said

Pink-Whistle. 'For instance, I can make myself disappear – like this!'

And lo and behold, he was gone! Absolutely gone! Derek stared in amazement. Then he gave a shout. 'Oh! I know who you are! Of course – you're Mr Pink-Whistle, aren't you, the little man who goes about the world putting wrong things right? Of course, of course!'

'Quite right,' said Mr Pink-Whistle, appearing again, much to the astonishment of a passing dog. 'Well now – I think we could do a marvellous show between us, don't you agree?'

'Oh *yes*!' said Derek, his eyes shining with excitement. 'Yes, yes, yes – a thousand yesses! What shall we do?'

'Come into the garage,' said Mr Pink-Whistle. 'We'll make a few plans.'

Well, the two of them disappeared into the garage and shut the doors, and what a lot of exciting plans they made.

'I'm bringing my cat Sooty tomorrow afternoon, as you know,' said Pink-Whistle, 'and he'll do anything we say. We'll make him perform as well, shall we?'

Derek could hardly sleep that night for excitement. He tossed and turned, thinking of all the tricks and magic he and Mr Pink-Whistle would do the next day. What fun it was going to be!

The next morning came at last and Derek set out rows of chairs and benches in the garage, and borrowed some big boxes from the greengrocer for the audience to sit on as well. The notice was back on the gate, of course, and Derek was busy selling tickets all morning. Tom, the mean boy from down the road, who had stolen the conjuring set, was most surprised to see that the show was still going to be given. He stood looking in at the garage, puzzled.

'Ha – come to bring back my conjuring set?' said Derek, spotting him.

'Who says I took it?' said the boy sullenly. 'You and your silly conjuring set! I'll come this afternoon, see if I don't, and spoil your show, for saying I took your set!'

'You'd better not,' said Derek in alarm. He simply couldn't have anything go wrong this afternoon!

At three o'clock the garage was full, and there were quite a lot of children standing at the back. Derek was very pleased to see how many tickets had been sold. He and Mr Pink-Whistle had made a slightly raised platform of planks at the end of the garage, and on it was a table with a black cloth over it, and a silver wand lying across it. On a stool lay the things that Derek was going to use at the show – a top hat borrowed from his father, several hankies, some new-laid eggs and other things.

Mr Pink-Whistle was there, but no one could see him because he had made himself quite invisible. Sooty his cat was there too, looking extremely smart with a red bow round his neck and one on his tail. He was very excited.

At three o'clock Derek walked on to the little platform and bowed. His mother had made him a cloak out of an old black velvet curtain, and lined it with red, and he looked very grand. He bowed to the clapping audience.

'Thank you for coming here,' he said. 'I will now begin my show which, I hope, will help to buy old Mrs Jordan a wheelchair. You will see marvellous things this afternoon, magical things that will puzzle you and fill you with wonder. But first I must introduce to you my helper – a black cat. As you know, witches have black cats and I, being a conjurer, must have one too. Sooty, bow to the audience.'

And to everyone's immense astonishment Sooty came on to the little platform and bowed graciously to everyone. They could hardly believe their eyes. A cat bowing! Whatever next?

Well, it turned out to be a perfectly marvellous afternoon. First Derek did the fly-away trick.

'I will show you my fly-away magic,' he said. 'See, I will put on my father's top hat – and when I tell it to fly away, it will do so! Watch!'

He put on the top hat and waved his wand. 'Hat! Fly away!' he cried. And hey presto, the hat rose into the air and flew gracefully all round the stage! When Derek shouted 'Come back, hat!' it came back to his head.

Of course, it was really the invisible Mr Pink-Whistle who had taken the hat off Derek's head, and run all round the stage with it, holding it high in his hand, and then popped the hat back on Derek's head. But as nobody could see Pink-Whistle, they thought the hat was flying all by itself!

'Now, hat – fly to my little cat-attendant,' shouted Derek, and at once the hat shot off his head and went to Sooty. It was far too big for him, of course, and everyone roared to see him trying to get it off his nose!

'Make the hat fly to *my* head!' cried a girl in the front row of the audience. In a flash the hat was off Sooty's head, and flying through the air to the girl's head. How she screamed for joy at such magic! It was really just Pink-Whistle, of course, taking the hat to her, unseen.

'Wonderful!' shouted the audience. 'Do some more tricks. Make the cat do something.'

'Sooty – please dance and sing!' commanded Derek, and Sooty at once began to do a comical little dance – and behind him, still invisible, Mr Pink-Whistle sang a wonderful song, each verse ending with 'Mee-OW, mee-OW, mee-OW.' All the audience joined in of course. How they clapped little Sooty!

'And now I will make anything belonging to you members of the audience disappear into thin air!' cried Derek. 'Who will bring up a handkerchief – or a book – or a purse? Don't be afraid, you'll get them all back.'

Harry came up with a comic. John came up with a bag of sweets. Beth came with a red hanky. Derek took them all.

'Stand by me,' he said. 'Now, Beth – throw your hanky into the air, please.'

Beth threw it up – and it disappeared! Yes, it absolutely vanished. No wonder it did, for the unseen Pink-Whistle had neatly caught it and stuffed it into his pocket, where it promptly disappeared. Then Harry threw up his comic and that vanished too. So did John's bag of sweets. It was too mysterious for words!

'I want my sweets back,' said John, looking all round. 'Where are they?'

'You will find your sweets and Harry's comic and Beth's hanky under the top hat on the table,' said Derek. And sure enough, when Harry ran and lifted up the top hat, there were the three things in a neat pile. The invisible Mr Pink-Whistle had slipped them there, of course.

'How do you do it? Derek, tell us how you do these marvellous tricks!' cried everyone, and even the grown-ups in the audience turned to one another, puzzled. How could a boy do such magical things?

Well, Derek did plenty more tricks, with the help of the unseen Mr Pink-Whistle, and of course Sooty the cat, who was enjoying himself immensely, and kept doing comical little dances all round the stage. He made the children laugh till they cried.

The most puzzling trick of all Derek kept till the last. 'Now,' he said, 'I want some of you to feel in your pockets and tell me if anything is missing. Put your hands up, if you are missing something.'

Everyone felt in their pockets and then hand after hand shot up. 'My notebook's missing!' 'My hanky's not here!' 'Hey – my wallet's gone!' 'I say – where's my penknife?'

'Come up on to the platform, please, all those who have lost something,' said Derek solemnly. 'I will get them back for you.'

They all filed up on to the stage – three children and two puzzled grown-ups. 'Stand in a line please,' said Derek. 'Now you, Mr Welsh – what have you lost?'

'My wallet,' said Mr Welsh anxiously.

'Hold out your hand, and I will send it back to you,' said Derek, and waved his wand as Mr Welsh promptly held out his hand.

Plonk! A wallet fell into his open palm at once! Mr Welsh stood there, amazed, unable to say a word. 'Why – it came right out of the air!' said the boy next to him. 'This is real magic!'

It wasn't, of course. It was just that Mr Pink-Whistle had walked quietly round the audience for a minute or two before, unseen, and taken this and that – and now, when the five people stood on the stage and asked for their things back, he simply dropped them into their waiting hands! It looked exactly as if they had fallen right out of the air. Derek kept waving his wand each time the lost things appeared, and the audience really and truly thought that he was sending their belongings back to them in some very mysterious way.

'And now,' said Derek, 'I've lost something. I've lost my conjuring set! Will the boy who took it from me please come up here?'

Tom, who had stolen it, sat trembling in his seat. Go up on the stage? Not he! Then he felt an invisible someone taking hold of his collar and forcing him to his feet. The someone pushed him firmly up to the stage and stood him there, facing the audience. How he shook and shivered!

'Ah – so it was you, Tom, who took my conjuring set!' said Derek sternly.

'I'll bring it back! I will, I promise I will!' said the terrified Tom. 'Who's holding me? Someone's got hold of my shirt collar. Let me go!'

'Very well. You can go. Bring back my conjuring set this evening – and empty your moneybox and bring the money to me, to help towards the wheelchair!' bellowed Derek suddenly, making everyone jump, Tom most of all. Pink-Whistle let go of his collar, and Tom disappeared out of the garage at top speed. Yes, yes – he would certainly give back the conjuring set, and every penny he had in his moneybox, if only Derek would never play magic tricks on him again!

The audience clapped and clapped. Some of them

even put more money into the box at the garage entrance as they went out. What a show!

'A black cat for an attendant – a cat that danced!' they said. 'Things disappearing and flying through the air! Whenever Derek waved his hand, something marvellous happened!'

Derek was very, very pleased with the afternoon's work. Mr Pink-Whistle made himself visible again, and they really couldn't help hugging one another.

'Grand, wasn't it?' said Pink-Whistle, chuckling. 'I never enjoyed myself so much in all my life. How much money have you taken?'

'Good gracious! More than fifty pounds!' said Derek, amazed. 'Mr Pink-Whistle, you must have put some in too, using your magic!'

Sooty the cat was very sorry it was all over. He and Pink-Whistle went to have tea with Derek's parents, and everyone was very happy indeed. Next week they are all going together to buy the wheelchair, because at last there is enough money.

I wish Mr Pink-Whistle would grant me a wish and let me come to the next conjuring show he helps with! I'd really love to be there!

Tick-Tock's Tea Party

Tick-Tock's Tea Party

TICK-TOCK THE ELF lived with the enchanter Wind-Whistle, and kept his house neat and tidy for him. He cooked his meals, washed his clothes, and sometimes he helped Wind-Whistle with his spells. He was hard at work all day long, but he was very happy.

One afternoon there came a knock at the door and Tick-Tock went to open it. Outside stood the Princess of the Blue Hills and two of her court, come to visit the enchanter and take his advice.

It was just teatime and Tick-Tock knew they would all stay to tea – and oh, dear me – there were no cakes at all, hardly any jam and just a pinch of tea!

'Pray come inside!' said Tick-Tock, bowing low, for he knew his manners very well. The princess came in, smelling very sweet and looking very lovely. Tick-Tock gave her and the ladies-in-waiting some chairs in the drawing room and went to tell Wind-Whistle of his royal visitor. All the time he was worrying about tea. What should he do for cakes and jam? You couldn't give royal princesses plain bread and butter – and goodness gracious, there was hardly any butter either! It was very worrying.

Wind-Whistle was pleased to hear of his royal visitor. He put on his best cloak at once and said to Tick-Tock, 'Get tea ready. Lay it nicely.'

'Oh, your highness, isn't it dreadful, there are no cakes, just a pinch of tea, hardly any jam and not much butter!' said poor Tick-Tock.

'Well, go to the shops and get some,' said the enchanter snappily.

'But they're shut this afternoon,' said Tick-Tock. 'It's early closing day!'

'Dear, dear, so it is,' said the enchanter. 'Well, never mind. Now listen carefully, Tick-Tock. Lay the table as usual, but place the butter dish, the jam dish, and cake dishes empty on the table – empty, do you hear? Put no tea in the teapot, but fill it with boiling water. I have a mind to do a little magic for the princess, and at the same time provide a good tea for her.'

Tick-Tock listened open-mouthed. How exciting!

He hurried to do what he was told. He laid the table, put out empty butter, jam and cake dishes, and filled the teapot with boiling water. Then he told the enchanter that everything was ready.

Wind-Whistle led the princess and her ladies into the room where the tea was laid and bade them be seated. They were surprised to see nothing to eat.

'Madam, do you like pale or dark tea?' began the enchanter, holding up the teapot. Then he caught sight of Tick-Tock peeping in at the door to watch everything.

'Go to the kitchen!' he ordered. 'And shut this door, Tick-Tock.'

Poor Tick-Tock! He had so badly wanted to see everything. He shut the door and went to the kitchen – but in half a minute he was back again, peeping through the keyhole and listening to what the enchanter was saying!

'I'll have the pale tea,' said the princess.

'Pale tea, pour forth!' commanded the enchanter, and the princess gave a scream of delight, for pale tea poured from the teapot into her cup.

'I'd like dark tea,' said each of her ladies, and when Wind-Whistle said, 'Dark tea, pour forth!' at once dark tea poured into their cups.

'What sort of jam do you like?' asked Wind-Whistle.

'Strawberry, please,' answered his three royal visitors.

'Strawberry jam, appear in the dish!' cried Wind-Whistle. Immediately a great heap of delicious jam appeared.

'And what cakes do you prefer?' asked the enchanter.

'Chocolate cakes for me!' cried the princess in excitement.

'Cherry buns for me!' said the first lady.

'And ginger fingers for me!' begged the second lady.

'Chocolate cakes, appear!' commanded the enchanter, tapping a dish. 'Cherry buns, come forth, ginger fingers, appear!'

Three dishes were suddenly full of the most delicious-looking cakes, and the ladies cried out in delight. Then the enchanter struck the butter dish.

'Now, butter, where are you?' he cried. Golden butter at once gleamed in the dish. It was marvellous. Outside the door Tick-Tock listened to all this, and tried to see through the keyhole what was happening. It was most exciting.

After tea Wind-Whistle called Tick-Tock to him.

'I'm going to the Blue Hills with the princess and her ladies,' he said. 'She needs my help. Look after my house and see that nothing goes wrong. And don't meddle with any magic or you will be sorry!'

By six o'clock Wind-Whistle and the ladies were gone and Tick-Tock was left alone. He finished up the cakes that were left from tea and enjoyed them very much. They were much nicer than any that were sold in the shops.

It was while he was eating the cakes that the naughty idea came to him. He clapped his hands for joy and danced round the kitchen.

'Why shouldn't I give a tea party and make all the cakes and things appear!' he shouted. 'I can wear the enchanter's magic cloak, and then all the things I say will come true too. Oh, how lovely! Won't I make everyone stare! My friends will think *I'm* an enchanter.'

He sat down at once and wrote six notes to his friends. One went to Big-Eyes, one to Little Feet, another to Pippity, the fourth to Gobo, and the last two to Pop and Tiptoe.

'Please come to a Magic Tea Party,' he wrote to each

of them. Then he licked up the envelopes and posted the letters. How excited he felt!

He had asked his friends for the next day. So he was very busy in the morning making the house tidy and putting fresh flowers on the tea table. Then after his dinner he washed himself, did his hair nicely, laid the tea table with empty plates and dishes, and at last went to put on the enchanter's magic cloak. It was embroidered with suns and moons and shone very brightly.

Tick-Tock walked about in front of the looking-glass in Wind-Whistle's bedroom and thought he looked really very grand.

'Won't I surprise everyone this afternoon!' he chuckled to himself. 'Dear me! There's the clock striking half past three! I must put the kettle on for tea.'

He ran downstairs, nearly tripping over the cloak he wore, for it was much too big for him. He put the kettle on, and waited for his friends.

They all came together, looking very smart in their best clothes. They were most excited and crowded round Tick-Tock, asking him what a Magic Tea Party was.

'Wait and see, wait and see!' said Tick-Tock, laughing.

He led them into the dining room, where tea was laid – but when they saw the empty dishes their faces grew long. Wasn't there going to be anything to eat?

'Wait and see, wait and see!' laughed Tick-Tock again, running into the kitchen to fetch the kettle, which was now boiling.

His guests sat down round the table, and waited. Tick-Tock came back with the kettle. He was going to do better than the enchanter – he was going to make the cakes, jam, butter and tea all appear at once!

'What sort of cakes and jam do you like?' he asked his guests. They all called out together.

'Gooseberry jam! Chocolate roll! Coconut buns! Cherry cake! Plum jam! Marmalade! Sponge fingers!'

'Right!' said Tick-Tock. He picked up the teapot, which he had filled with nothing but hot water, and then cried out loudly, 'Tea, pour forth! Butter, appear! Gooseberry jam, plum jam, marmalade, where are you? Chocolate roll, coconut buns, cherry cake, sponge fingers, come forth!'

Then, to the enormous surprise of all his friends, the teapot poured tea into their cups, one after another, jam and marmalade began to come into the dishes, butter heaped itself up in another dish, and cakes fell into a pile on the rest of the dishes. It was perfectly marvellous!

'Wonderful!' cried Gobo.

'How do you do it!' shouted Pop and Tiptoe.

'Goodness gracious!' cried the others.

'It's easy!' said Tick-Tock, pouring out his cup of tea last of all. 'I'm quite a good magician, you know. I'm sure I could teach Wind-Whistle a lot.'

A puzzled look came over the faces of the six guests as they watched the jam, butter and cakes appearing in the dishes. They had been appearing for quite a while now, and the dishes were much too full. In fact the gooseberry jam was spilling on to the cloth.

'You ought to have put out bigger dishes,' said Tiptoe to Tick-Tock. 'Look, they aren't big enough for all the cakes and things.'

But Tick-Tock was also feeling puzzled about something and didn't hear what Tiptoe said. The teapot had filled his cup, but when he set it down on the teapot stand, it didn't stay there. No, it hopped up into the air all by itself and began to pour tea into the milk jug! It was most peculiar. Tick-Tock took hold of it and put it back on the tray. But as soon as he let go, up hopped the teapot into the air again and poured a stream of tea into the sugar basin. It was most annoying.

'I say, Tick-Tock, the dishes aren't *big* enough, I tell you!' said Tiptoe as he and the others watched the cakes spilling all over the table. 'Shall we get some more?'

'No, just help yourselves and eat as much as you

want to,' said Tick-Tock, still busy with the obstinate teapot. 'If you eat up the cakes there will soon be room for them on the dishes.'

So the guests began eating – but, dear me, they couldn't eat nearly as fast as those cakes, jams and butter appeared! Soon the tablecloth was in a dreadful mess, for the jam slid over the edge of the pot and dripped on to the table, and the butter flopped down too, while the marmalade was in big blobs all round its dish. The cakes no longer fell on the dishes as they appeared out of the air, but bounced straight on to the table, scattering crumbs all over the place.

The guests were rather frightened, especially when they saw what trouble the teapot was giving poor Tick-Tock. But they said no more.

They ate steadily, though nothing really tasted very nice. Poor Tick-Tock could eat nothing, for all the time he was trying to stop the teapot from pouring tea here, there and everywhere.

At last it tore itself away from the frightened elf and poured some tea down Gobo's neck!

'Ow!' squealed Gobo, jumping up in fright as the hot tea dripped down his collar. 'Ow! Ooh! It's burnt me!'

He wiped the tea away with his handkerchief and began to cry.

'Hoo, hoohoo! I'm going home! This isn't a nice tea party.'

He ran out of the door and slammed it. The others looked at one another. The teapot moved towards Tiptoe, but he jumped out of the way.

'Goodbye, Tick-Tock,' he said. 'I must get home. I've some work to do.'

'I must go with him,' said Pop, and the two elves ran off in a hurry.

It wasn't long before the other guests went too. The magic was frightening them. It was all very well to have as many cakes as you wanted, but to see hundreds dropping on to the table was very peculiar. They felt sure something had gone wrong.

Tick-Tock was very unhappy and rather frightened. What had happened? Hadn't he done the magic just the same as Wind-Whistle? Why wouldn't everything stop appearing? Why didn't that horrid teapot stop pouring?

Tick-Tock looked round the table in despair. What a mess! Look at all the jam and marmalade! Look at those cakes, not even bothering to fall on the dishes any more! Look at the butter all over the place! And look at that perfect nuisance of a teapot pouring tea on the carpet now! Whatever was he to do?

Poor Tick-Tock! He couldn't do anything. He had started a magic that he couldn't stop. The teapot suddenly stopped pouring tea on the carpet and playfully poured some on Tick-Tock's beautiful cloak. He cried out in dismay.

'Oh! Look what you've done to the enchanter's best cloak! Oh, what a mess! Whatever will he say? Oh, my goodness me, I must go and sponge off the tea at once!'

Tick-Tock rushed upstairs to the bathroom. He

took a sponge and began to sponge the tea stain on the cloak. He was dreadfully afraid the enchanter would see it, and what would he say then? Oh, dear, dear, why ever had Tick-Tock meddled with magic when he had been told not to?

It took a long time to get the tea stain out of the cloak, but at last it was done. Tick-Tock hung the cloak over a chair to dry and was just going downstairs when he heard someone shouting from outside the house. He stuck his head out of the window to see what the matter was.

Out of doors stood Gobo, and he was shouting at the top of his voice.

'Hi, Tick-Tock! Are you all right? There are a lot of funny things happening down here! Look!'

Tick-Tock looked – and out of the front door he saw a stream of tea flowing! Yes, really, it was running down the path! Mixed with it was butter, jam, marmalade and cakes of all kinds, bobbing up and down in the stream.

'Oooooh!' screamed Tick-Tock, and ran downstairs in a hurry. Well! I couldn't tell you what the dining room looked like. It was a foot deep in tea, to begin with, for the teapot was still pouring away merrily. And then the cakes! Well, there were hundreds and hundreds of them. The jam and marmalade and butter were all mixed up together, and still more and more things were dropping down into the room.

Tick-Tock waded in. The teapot at once poured some tea on his nose and he gave a cry of pain, for it was hot. Whatever was he to do? This was dreadful.

'Can't you stop the things coming and coming and coming?' shouted Gobo, who was really very sorry for his friend. 'You made them start.'

'I know,' sobbed Tick-Tock. 'But I thought they would stop by themselves and they haven't. If only Wind-Whistle was here!'

Then Gobo gave a shout and pointed up the street. 'Here he comes!' he cried. 'He's come home sooner than you thought!'

So he had. Poor Tick-Tock! He didn't know whether to be glad or sorry. Wind-Whistle strode up the road and when he came to his house and saw the stream of tea pouring out, mixed with jam and cakes, he was most astonished. He stared at it in amazement, while poor Tick-Tock tried to stammer all about it.

'What! You dared to meddle with magic when I told you not to!' shouted the enchanter in anger. 'You wore my magic cloak! How dare you?'

'Oh, please, your highness, forgive me!' wept the elf, as white as a sheet. 'I just thought I would give a tea party like you did. It looked so easy. But nothing would stop. It just went on and on. The teapot is still pouring in the dining room.'

The enchanter waded through the stream of tea and looked in at the dining room door. What a dreadful sight! He frowned in anger. Then he clapped his hands sharply three times and said, 'Illa rimmytooma lippitty crim!' These words were so magic that Tick-Tock trembled to hear them. But at the sound of them the teapot at once stopped its pouring and put itself in the sink to be washed up. The cakes stopped falling from the air, and so did the jam, marmalade and butter.

But the dreadful mess remained. Tick-Tock looked at it in despair.

'Aren't you going to make all this mess go too?' he asked his master.

'No, *you're* going to make that go!' said Wind-Whistle sternly. 'Get brushes, cloths, soap and water, Tick-Tock, and clear it up. It will keep you busy.'

Tick-Tock went away howling. The mess would take him days to clear up. But it was his own fault, he shouldn't have meddled with magic. He never would again, never!

Wind-Whistle forgave Tick-Tock, when the house was clean and tidy again. But when he wants to tease the little elf he says, 'Would you like another tea party, Tick-Tock, some day?'

But Tick-Tock shakes his head and cries, 'No, no, no. Never again!'

The Fly-Away Cottage

The Fly-Away Cottage

JOANNA AND PAUL looked out of the nursery window. It was pouring with rain, and they had to go across the fields to fetch the eggs from the farm.

'What a nuisance!' said Paul. 'It's such a long way down the road and over the hill to the farm when it's raining.'

'Well, let's take the short cut through the woods,' said Joanna. 'We can put on our big rubber boots and our mackintoshes and sou'westers, and we shall be sheltered from the wind if we walk through the wood. It won't take us very long.'

So they put on their rubber boots, and their mackintoshes and oilskin hats. They took the basket for the eggs, called goodbye to their mother and set out. It *was* raining hard! There were big puddles everywhere, and the rain splashed into them and made them bigger still! The wind blew hard too, and altogether it was a very stormy, windy day.

Soon the two children came to the woods. They were glad to get among trees, for they were more sheltered then. They walked through the dripping trees, over the soaking grass. Then suddenly came such a gale blustering through the woods that the children were quite frightened.

'I hope the wind won't blow any trees down on us,' said Joanna, looking round at the trees bent almost double in the gale. 'I wish there was somewhere for us to shelter in just until this storm is over, Paul. Is there any cottage near that we could go to?'

'No,' said Paul. 'I've never seen any cottage here at all.'

Just as he spoke, Joanna cried out in surprise and pointed to the left.

'Look, Paul! There's the funniest cottage I've ever seen. What are those things growing out of each side of it?'

It certainly was a strange cottage. Jutting out at each side of it were big feathery wings. They were perfectly still, and drooped a little in the rain. The cottage was very small, and had a yellow front door with one chimney that twisted here and there in the wind.

'It's the funniest cottage I've ever seen,' said Paul. 'I don't know whether to go to it or not. It looks odd to me. Goodness knows who might live there – a witch perhaps, or an enchanter. It's just the sort of cottage you see in a book.'

The two children stood looking at it, and the rain fell more and more heavily on them.

'It's raining cats and dogs,' said Paul, and, my goodness me, just as he said that, his words came true. It really *did* begin to rain cats and dogs! A large black kitten fell on Joanna's head, and a little white dog fell down by Paul. Then two tabby cats tumbled near Joanna and three collies around Paul. The children stood looking at them in amazement. Then they looked up at the sky. It was full of cats and dogs, all falling to earth like rain!

'Quick! Run to the cottage!' said Paul in a fright. 'We don't want hundreds of dogs and cats on our heads! It must be a very bad storm if it rains cats and dogs!'

So they ran through the falling cats and dogs to the funny little cottage. Joanna thought she saw its wings move a little as they came near. A black cat fell on to her shoulder and made her squeal. She rushed to the cottage door and turned the handle. She and Paul ran inside and slammed the door behind them.

A smell of newly made cakes was in the cottage. The children gazed around the room they were in. A small woman with green wings growing out of her shoulders looked round at them from the fireplace.

'Now then, now then, what do you mean by rushing in like that without so much as a knock at the door or a ring?' she said grumpily. 'Here I've got my oven door open and my cakes are baking as well, and you come in and make a draught like that. It's enough to make them all go flat, so it is.'

The children were so surprised to see such a funny person that they couldn't speak. The woman was short and round and she wore a sort of sunbonnet on her head. Her cheeks were hot from the fire, and she shut her oven door with a slam.

'Well?' she said. 'Haven't you a tongue in your heads, either of you? What do you want? Have you come to buy any of my cakes?'

'No,' said Paul. 'We didn't know you sold them. Are you a fairy?'

'I'm a pixie woman,' said the funny little person, taking off her spectacles and polishing them on her big white apron. 'I'm the famous Mother Mickle-Muckle, whose cakes are bought for all the best parties in

Fairyland and Witchland. Haven't you ever heard of me?'

'No,' said Joanna, feeling rather excited to see a real pixie person. 'I'm so sorry if our opening the door has spoilt your cakes. But, you see, it's raining cats and dogs outside and we had to run for shelter.'

'Cats and dogs!' said the pixie woman in surprise. 'Nonsense!'

Just as she spoke a large brown and white dog fell down the chimney into the fire. It jumped out at once and ran barking round the kitchen. Mother Mickle-Muckle picked up a frying-pan and ran after it.

'Get out, you clumsy creature!' she said. 'I won't have animals in my nice clean kitchen!'

She opened the door and the dog ran out into the wood. But no sooner had the pixie woman shut it than two big cats fell down her chimney, and when they had jumped out on the hearth rug they began to fight, spitting and snarling at one another in a spiteful manner. The pixie picked up a rolling pin and rushed angrily at the cats.

They flew at her and scratched her on the hand. Then out of the window they jumped, still hissing at one another.

'Look at that now!' said Mother Mickle-Muckle, showing her hand to the children. 'I won't stay here a minute longer! I hate dogs and cats falling down my chimney! Cottage, fly to Topsy-Turvy Land!'

Before the children could say a word the cottage spread its two feathery wings and flew up into the air! Yes, it really did! Joanna rushed to a window and she saw its wings beating the air like a bird's, and, as she watched, the trees were left behind and the cottage rose high into the air.

'Ooh!' cried Joanna in the greatest astonishment. 'The cottage is flying away!'

'Of course,' said the pixie, busy rolling out some pastry on the kitchen table. 'It's Fly-Away Cottage, didn't you know that? It's famous all over the world.'

'Well, *I've* never heard of it,' said Joanna. 'Have you, Paul?'

'Never,' said Paul, looking in wonder out of the window, gazing at fields and woods below them.

'Then you are two silly, ignorant children,' said Mother Mickle-Muckle quite crossly. 'I don't know where you go to school, if they don't teach you things like that.'

'I wish we *were* taught things like that!' said Joanna. 'It would be much more exciting to learn about this Fly-Away Cottage, and you, than about bays and rivers.'

Mother Mickle-Muckle was pleased. She took a plate of chocolate buns from the cupboard and put them down in front of the children.

'You can each have two,' she said. 'We shan't arrive at Topsy-Turvy Land for another hour or two. Take off your coats and hats and sit down.'

'Whatever will Mother say if we don't go back for dinner?' said Paul. 'I don't think we ought to go to Topsy-Turvy Land, Mother Mickle-Muckle, though I'd love to.'

'You'll *have* to go,' said the pixie, popping another tin of cakes into the oven. 'I am taking some cakes to the Big Little Goblin for his party this afternoon and he would turn me into a biscuit or an ice cream if I were late.'

'Big Little Goblin!' said Joanna in surprise. 'Nobody can be big and little too.'

'Oh, can't they?' said Mother Mickle-Muckle, rolling out some more dough. 'Well, let me tell you, my clever girl, that the Big Little Goblin is little in height but very big in width. That is, he is very short and very round, and he is the king of Topsy-Turvy Land because he is the silliest person there.'

'Then why do they make him king?' asked Paul, astonished.

'Oh, everything is upside down in Topsy-Turvy Land,' said the pixie. 'The silliest is the king and the cleverest is a beggar. Now just sit down and keep quiet while I decorate these cakes. We'll be passing over the sea in a little while, and you can watch the ships.'

It was strange to be in a little cottage flying high above the clouds. The two children looked out of the windows and saw the ships on the sea, and then at last they were over land again. The cottage swooped down and landed with a bump on a little hill. The children were thrown off their feet, but Mother Mickle-Muckle didn't seem to mind.

She put some cakes into a basket and opened the door. 'Come along,' she said.

The children followed her – and how surprised they were to see the land they had come to. Everything was topsy-turvy!

The houses stood on their chimneys, and the people had to have ladders to get up to their front doors. It was really most peculiar. The people walked the right way up but they all wore a large boot or shoe on their heads instead of a hat. Joanna and Paul wanted to laugh whenever they met anyone.

The people were mostly small and round, and they all had funny little button noses and pointed ears. They wore their coats back to front and they talked very loudly in high voices.

The Big Little Goblin lived in a small cottage and didn't look a bit like a king. He wore a red button-boot on his head, and round one of his legs was a golden crown. He took the basket of cakes from Mother Mickle-Muckle and peered at them to see if they were all right.

'He's a funny sort of king,' said Joanna, when they came out of the cottage. 'I should have thought he would have lived in that big palace over there.' She pointed to a high, shining palace a little way off.

'Oh, that's where the cleverest man lives, the beggar I told you of,' said the pixie woman. 'This is Topsy-Turvy Land, remember. Beggars live in palaces and kings live in cottages.'

Joanna stopped to watch a Topsy-Turvy Man walk up the ladder to his upside-down front door. She thought it must be very funny to walk on ceilings and see your fire burning upside down.

'Come along, come along,' said Mother Mickle-Muckle impatiently. 'I must get to Giant Too-Tall's before one o'clock with a jam roll.'

They hurried back to where the Fly-Away Cottage was waiting for them. It was waving its feathery wings in the air, and was so anxious to be away that it rose up in the air almost before Joanna had gone through the door. She nearly fell out as it rose with a jerk and Paul just caught her in time and pulled her into the kitchen.

'We'd better have our dinner while the cottage is flying to Giant Too-Tall's,' said the pixie woman, and she set the table with a white cloth. For their dinner she gave them hot ginger buns, cherry pie and cheese biscuits straight from the oven. They liked it very much. The cottage flew steadily through the air while they ate, and when next the children looked out of the window they saw a big dark cloud in front of them with something glittering in the middle of it.

'There's a castle right in the middle of the cloud!' said Joanna in surprise. 'Goodness, how wonderful!'

Sure enough, there was! The cottage flew into the thick cloud and set itself down in the castle yard. The pixie woman took a small jam roll out of the oven.

'Is that for a giant?' asked Paul, laughing. 'Goodness, he must be a small giant!'

'You wait and see!' said Mother Mickle-Muckle, and she opened the door of her cottage.

'Coo-ee!' she called, in a high, bird-like voice. 'Coo-ee!'

The door of the great castle opened and out came an enormously tall giant with eyes as big as dinner plates. Joanna and Paul felt quite frightened and ran back into the cottage.

'Have you brought my jam roll?' called a thundering voice and the cottage shook from top to bottom.

'Yes, come and get it,' answered the pixie woman and she held out the jam roll she had made. The children saw a big hand come down to get it and, dear me, what a very peculiar thing happened! As soon as the jam roll touched the giant's hand, it grew ten times as large, and was the biggest jam roll the children had ever seen in their lives!

'Thanks,' said the giant's booming voice, and he gave the pixie woman a coin as large as a saucer. But as soon as it touched her hand it became small, and she slipped it in her pocket.

'Have you got visitors in your Fly-Away Cottage?' suddenly asked the giant and he bent down and looked through one of the windows. 'Ho, children! Come along with me and play with my daughter!'

'Good gracious me, no!' cried the pixie woman. 'She would think they were dolls and would break them in a second.'

'You give them to *me*!' said the giant and he tried to open the window to get at the children. But the pixie woman called out, 'Fly away, cottage, to the cave of the elf!'

The cottage at once spread its wings and left the

dark cloud with its great castle towering in the midst. It flew into the blue sky, and the two children were delighted to leave the tall giant behind.

The cottage flew lazily along, and the pixie woman looked at the clock. It said three o'clock. She tapped sharply on the wall of the cottage and cried, 'Now then, Fly-Away Cottage, hurry up or we shan't be at the elf's cave in time for tea. He must have his cherry buns for it's his birthday party.'

The cottage began to flap its wings so fast that it jerked about and the children sat down suddenly on the floor. Cups flew off the dresser and a chair fell on to the pixie woman's toe so that she cried out in pain.

'Now, now,' she shouted, banging at the cottage wall with her rolling pin, 'what are you thinking of, cottage, to fly so fast? Be sensible. We don't want to be jerked out of the windows.' They were passing over the sea again, but it was a very odd sea, for it was bright yellow, streaked with pink.

Time went on and soon the hands of the clock

pointed to four. A mountain came in sight, standing right up in the middle of the yellow sea, just like a pointed island. The cottage flew to it and perched on the very top. The children wondered if it would slide down – and no sooner did they wonder it than the cottage *did* slide down! What a funny feeling it was – just like going down in a very swift lift!

Bump! The cottage reached the bottom and the children fell over again. When they picked themselves up they saw the pixie woman going out of the door with a basket of cherry buns.

'Don't come with me,' she said. 'The Tick-Tock Elf is bad-tempered and might want to keep you for servants. Stay here.'

So the children stayed where they were, and peeped out of the door. Joanna saw a strange-looking flower growing not far off and ran out to get it. As she stooped to pick it she heard a voice say, 'Ha! Here are some children! Let's take them prisoners!'

She looked up and saw a tiny elf staring at her, and

not far away were about a dozen others like him. They all had long beards reaching to the ground, and wore long, pointed shoes on their big feet. Joanna was frightened and she ran back to the cottage and slammed the door, hoping that the pixie woman would return very soon.

But she didn't come. The elves surrounded the cottage and came closer and closer. Paul locked the door and fastened all the windows.

'I believe there's an elf coming down the chimney!' he said suddenly, and sure enough, there was!

'They'll capture us!' said Joanna, looking ready to cry. Paul peeped out of the window to see if the pixie woman was coming but there was no sign of her.

So in despair he cried out to the cottage, 'Fly-Away Cottage, please fly away from here and take us home!'

At once, the cottage spread its wings and rose into the air! The children were so glad. The elf who was climbing down the chimney got out again in a great hurry and jumped to the ground just in time. The cottage flew over the yellow and pink sea at a great pace. Joanna and Paul were glad to leave the elves' island but they were worried about the pixie woman. What would she do? Would she have to live on the island all her life?

Suddenly they heard a cross voice shouting. They looked out of the window. Behind them flew the pixie woman trying her hardest to keep up with the cottage.

'Open the door and let me in!' she shouted. 'You silly children, open the door.'

They opened the door, and Mother Mickle-Muckle flew in. She sat down by the fire and panted. She was very cross with them.

'Flying off with my cottage like that!' she said. 'I never heard of such a thing! I shall take you both straight back home. I really don't know what you'll do next!'

The children were *so* glad to be flying home. They had had quite enough adventures for one day. Just as the clock hands pointed to twenty past four the cottage flew downwards, and the children saw that they were in their very own garden! How glad they were! It had stopped raining, and the sun was shining. They took up their mackintoshes and hats and stepped out of the strange Fly-Away Cottage.

'Goodbye, Mother Mickle-Muckle,' they said. 'Thank you for our nice dinner and all the adventures.'

'You're welcome to them,' said the little pixie woman, putting another tin of cakes into her oven and slamming the door. 'Come and see me again when it's raining cats and dogs!'

Off they ran and the last they saw of the Fly-Away Cottage was a speck in the air that looked like a kite as the cottage flapped away to the west where the sun was sinking slowly. 'I *do* hope we see it again if ever it rains cats and dogs,' said Joanna. I'd like to too, wouldn't you?

Winkle Makes a Mistake

Winkle Makes a Mistake

WINKLE WAS A mean and dishonest old gnome. If he found a bad coin he pretended it was a good one and gave it to a shopkeeper on a dark evening. If he could borrow anything and not return it, he did. His house was quite full of basins, brooms and plates he had borrowed and never taken back!

'You'll be sorry one day!' said the people who knew him. 'Yes, you will! People like you don't get on well in this world!'

But Winkle only grinned – for he really got on very well indeed. He had a long red stocking put away full of money. He always had chicken every Saturday for dinner, which his black cat caught for him from the farm over the hill, and he always had warm clothes to wear in winter.

'I get on all right!' he said to himself. 'What's the sense of being honest if it keeps you poor? No, no – I'll go my own way and be rich!'

So he went on being mean and dishonest, and getting richer and richer.

Now one day he went shopping in the next town. He bought all kinds of things, and asked the shops to send them home to him. The only parcel he took home was a brown paper one with his mended shoes inside.

He caught the bus and sat down. Next to him was a very smart fellow, a gnome who lived in a big castle in the next village to Winkle. He took no notice of Winkle at all, although the gnome said, 'Good morning.' He didn't like the look of Winkle, it was plain.

Winkle got out at his village, picked up the brown paper parcel and walked home, feeling very cross with the fine gnome who hadn't said 'Good morning' to him. He put down his parcel and put on the kettle to boil.

After he had had a cup of cocoa and some bread and cheese he opened his parcel to take out his mended old shoes – and what a surprise he got!

In the parcel was a pair of very fine shoes indeed – oh, very fine ones, fit for a king to wear! They were of leather sewn with gold, and had gold laces threaded through, and buckles set with pearls. Winkle stared at them in astonishment.

The old cobbler at the shop has put the wrong shoes in my parcel! he thought to himself. *Silly fellow! How careless of him! Well, I'm not going to bother to give them back to him. He shouldn't have been so silly as to make that mistake! I shall keep them and wear them! Ho, ho!*

Wasn't he mean? He ought to have taken them back at once to the cobbler, of course. He put them away in his cupboard and longed for a party so that he might wear them and be very grand indeed.

Now it wasn't the cobbler who had made the

mistake at all. He had put the right shoes in the gnome's parcel – Winkle's old mended ones. It was *Winkle* who had made a mistake – for in the bus he had sat next to the smart gnome who had also a parcel with him, and in *his* parcel was a pair of very fine shoes he had been to buy for His Majesty the king! Winkle hadn't looked to see that he was taking the right parcel when he jumped from the bus – he had picked up the parcel belonging to the other gnome and gone off with that.

So when the grand gnome arrived home and opened *his* parcel, what should he find but a pair of old mended shoes and he was most disgusted. He guessed at once what had happened. The other gnome in the bus, the one who had said 'Good morning' to him, must have taken the wrong parcel. Oh, well, it was annoying, but no doubt when the other fellow found out his mistake he would bring back the shoes.

But, of course, Winkle didn't. As you know, he put

them into his cupboard and kept them for himself, thinking that the cobbler had made a mistake.

Now when the grand gnome didn't get the shoes brought back, and found that nobody had asked the bus conductor about them, he decided to put up notices everywhere, to say what had happened, and to tell the gnome who had taken the wrong parcel where to bring the shoes. So he wrote some notices in red ink and stuck them up all over the place, in the villages around.

At the top of the notice he printed three words very large indeed. The words were 'GOLD-LACED SHOES'. Anyone catching sight of those words and having the wrong shoes at home would be sure to read the notice, thought the grand gnome, and he would soon have the shoes back.

Well, it wasn't long before Winkle the gnome did see those notices, and read the words at the top, 'GOLD-LACED SHOES'. But he didn't read any further.

It's only that silly cobbler putting up notices about the

shoes he gave me in mistake for my own, thought Winkle. *Well, if I don't read the notice, I can't find out anything more about the grand shoes, and as I don't* want *to find out anything, I shan't read the notice!*

So he didn't – and he was the only person in the village who didn't know that the shoes belonged to the king himself!

Well, when no one brought back the shoes to the grand gnome in his castle he became angry.

Someone is keeping them for himself! he thought. *Oho! Well, I can soon stop that! Shoes, come to me, and clatter as you come!*

Then a most extraordinary thing happened. Those gold-laced shoes, put safely away in Winkle's cupboard, began to struggle to get out. They wriggled out of the door and began to make a clatter on the floor. Winkle heard them and ran to see what was the matter.

When he saw that the shoes were trying to get away he was surprised and angry and put them back into the cupboard again.

But once more they struggled out, almost breaking the door down! They wriggled away from Winkle's hands and danced downstairs. They shot out of the front door with Winkle after them and clattered off down the street, making a great noise.

'Stop! Come back!' yelled Winkle, who wasn't going to lose those fine shoes if he could help it. But the shoes took no notice at all. They just went on, making a great clatter all the way down the street. Then people poured out of their houses to see the strange sight, and followed Winkle and the shoes, laughing and pointing. What an excitement for the village! Wherever were those shoes going?

The shoes went clattering to the next village and climbed up the steps of the castle where the grand gnome lived. He heard them coming and went to meet them. He saw behind them an angry gnome, trying in vain to catch hold of the dancing shoes.

'Take this man,' the big gnome ordered his servants. 'Bring him before me in my castle.'

He picked up the shoes, and strode inside, the servants following with the surprised Winkle between them. Winkle was truly amazed. Why was he suddenly being treated like this?

He stood before the grand gnome.

'How did you come by these shoes?' asked the gnome sternly.

'Oh – the c-c-cobbler put them into my parcel by m-m-mistake,' stammered Winkle in fright.

'Why didn't you take them back to him then?' said the gnome.

'Well, if he was silly enough to make a mistake I thought he should be punished for it,' said Winkle more boldly.

'I see,' said the gnome. 'You think if people make mistakes they deserve to be punished, even if they didn't mean to make them?'

'Certainly,' said Winkle.

'Well, listen to a little tale I have to tell of a gnome who made a big mistake,' said the grand gnome, in a stern voice. 'Once there were two gnomes in a bus, each with a brown-paper parcel. One gnome had old mended shoes in his parcel, but the other had gold-laced shoes he had bought for His Majesty the king. Now one of the gnomes got off the bus first and by mistake took the wrong parcel.'

Winkle grew pale. How dreadful! So it wasn't the cobbler's mistake after all – it was *he*, Winkle, who had made a mistake!

'As you have just said,' went on the grand gnome, 'a mistake must be punished, even though it was not made on purpose! You will go to prison, or pay a fine of ten shillings to the poor people of the villages around! Oh, Winkle, you think I have not heard of you and your mean, dishonest ways – but your name is known by everyone! You are rich – but only by wrongdoing! Now you shall be poor, and also by wrongdoing! Well – which is it to be – prison or ten shillings?'

'I haven't got ten shillings,' wailed Winkle. 'I've only seven in my long red stocking at home.'

'Bring me that,' said the gnome. 'And work hard and honestly for the rest, which you must bring to me as you earn it. And remember this, Winkle – riches got by ill means will sooner or later fly away, even as yours have done! Now go!'

Winkle stumbled home, sobbing and crying, to fetch his hoard of money. He was bitterly ashamed of himself. His neighbours pointed at him and nodded their heads.

'We told him so!' they whispered to one another. 'Meanness and dishonesty only come to one end!'

Poor Winkle! He is working hard every day now. His hoard of money is gone, and he is trying to earn more to make up the ten shillings. But he has learnt his lesson. If he borrows, he pays back. If he finds what isn't his, he gives it back to the owner at once. He doesn't cheat, he doesn't shirk. And it may be that by the time he has earned enough money to pay the ten shillings, he will be a different person – straight, honest and true.

I hope so, don't you?

The Little Clockwinder

The Little Clockwinder

DICKORY DOCK WAS the clockwinder to the king of Elfland. The king was very fond of clocks and he had a great many. He liked them all to show the same time, and to strike and chime exactly at the right minute. Dickory Dock was supposed to wind them each night – but, you know, he often didn't, and then the clocks went wrong.

One day the king gave him a little magic key. 'Look, Dickory Dock,' he said, 'here is an enchanted key that will wind up anything in the world, no matter what it is – but you, of course, must simply use it for clocks. Instead of keeping a hundred different keys, as you have always had to do, you may now throw them all away and use just this one for every clock in the palace.'

Dickory Dock was delighted – but, even though his work was now much easier, he didn't always remember to wind up the clocks. And one day the king was so cross that he scolded Dickory Dock.

Then wasn't Dickory Dock in a temper! How he vowed he would punish the king for scolding him! What a lot of rubbish he talked – and in the end, he thought of the naughtiest, silliest idea imaginable.

'I'll use my magic key and wind up everything in the palace!' he cried. Straight away he began to do this. He wound up every chair, big and small, every table, round or square, every stool and every bookcase. He even wound up the books, the vases and the cushions – and when the king and queen came home that night, what a strange and mysterious sight met their eyes!

'Bless us all!' cried the queen, as a table came dancing up to her. 'What's this!'

'Mercy on us!' shouted the king, as two chairs ran up to him and danced round him. 'What's happened!'

'Look at that stool!' cried the queen. 'It's dancing with my best red cushion! Everything's alive!'

'Dickory Dock has been using the magic key I gave him!' stormed the king in a rage. 'Get away, you clumsy great table, you're treading on my toe. Just look at those books rushing round the room! Where's Dickory Dock? Fetch him at once!'

Dickory Dock was hiding behind the door.

A footman peeped into the room when he heard the king shouting, and in a second he caught the mischievous clockwinder by the shoulder, and brought him before the king. Two or three cups came and ran round them, and a saucer rolled all the way up the stately footman's leg. It was really most peculiar.

'Go away from Elfland at once!' roared the king in a fury. 'Never come back! Give me your key, and I'll wind you up so you'll have to keep on walking and never stop. That will be a good punishment for you!'

With that he put the magic key into the mischievous elf and wound him up. Poor Dickory Dock! He started running off and it wasn't long before he came to our land. He has been here ever since. What do you suppose he does? He winds up the dandelion clocks, of course! He's just as careless over those as he used to be over the clocks in the palace, and that is why they are so seldom right! Puff one and see!

'Tell Me My Name!'

'Tell Me My Name!'

THE HOPPETTY GNOME lived in a little cottage all by himself. He kept no dog and no cat, but outside in the garden lived a freckled thrush who sang to Hoppetty each morning and evening to thank him for the crumbs he put out.

Hoppetty was very fond of this thrush. She was a pretty bird, and the songs she sang were very lovely.

'The sky is blue, blue!
And all day through, through,
I sing to you, you!'

That was the thrush's favourite song, and Hoppetty knew it by heart.

Now one day a dreadful thing happened. Hoppetty was trotting through the wood, going home after his shopping, when out pounced a big goblin and caught hold of him. He put Hoppetty into a sack and ran off with the struggling gnome over hill and meadow until he came to the tall hill on the top of which he lived. Then he emptied Hoppetty out of his sack, and told him he was to be his cook.

'I am very fond of cakes with jam inside,' said the grinning goblin, 'and I love chocolate fingers sprinkled with nuts. I have heard that you are a clever cake-maker. Make me these things.'

Poor Hoppetty! How he had to work! The goblin really had a most enormous appetite, and as he ate nothing but jam cakes and chocolate fingers, Hoppetty was busy all day long at the oven, baking, baking. He was always hot and always tired. He wondered and wondered who this strange goblin was, and one day he asked him.

'Who are you?' he said.

'Oho! Wouldn't you like to know?' said the goblin, putting six chocolate fingers into his mouth at once. 'Well, Hoppetty, if you could guess my name, I'd let you go. But you never will!'

Hoppetty sighed. He was sure he never *would* guess the goblin's name. Goblins had such strange names. Nobody ever came to the house, no letters were pushed through the letterbox, and Hoppetty was never allowed to go out. So how could he possibly find out the goblin's name? He tried a few guesses.

'Is your name Thingumebob?'

'Ho, ho, ho! No, no, no!'

'Is it Mankypetoddle?'

'Ho, ho, ho! No, no, no!'

'Well, is it Tiddleywinks?'

'Ho, ho, ho! No, no, no!'

Then Hoppetty sighed and set to work to make more

jam cakes, for the goblin had eaten twenty-two for breakfast, and the larder was getting empty.

The goblin went out and banged the door. He locked it too, and went down the path. Hoppetty knew he couldn't get out. He had tried before. The windows opened two inches, and no more. The door he couldn't open at all. He was indeed a prisoner. He sighed again and set to work quickly.

And then he heard something that made his heart leap. It was a bird singing sweetly.

'The sky is blue, blue!
And all day through, through,
I sing to you, you!'

It was his thrush! Hoppetty rushed to the window and looked out of the open crack. There was the pretty freckled bird, sitting in a nearby tree.

'Thrush!' cried Hoppetty. 'I'm here! Oh, you dear creature, have you been going about singing and looking for me? Did you miss your crumbs? I'm a prisoner here. I can only get away if I find out the name of the goblin who keeps me here.'

Just then the goblin came back, and the gnome rushed to his baking once more. The thrush sang sweetly outside for a few minutes and then flew away.

The bird was unhappy. It loved Hoppetty. The gnome had been so kind to her, and had loved her singing so very much. If only the thrush could find out the name of the goblin. But how?

The bird made up her mind to watch the goblin and see where he went. So the next day she followed him when he left the cottage, flying from tree to tree as the goblin went on his way. At last he came to another cottage, and, to the thrush's surprise, the door was opened by a black cat with bright green eyes.

A witch cat! thought the thrush. *I wonder if she knows the goblin's name. I dare not ask her, for if I go too near she will spring at me.*

The goblin stayed a little while and then went away.

The thrush was about to follow, when the cat brought out a spinning wheel and set it in the sunshine by the door. She sat down and began to spin her wool.

And as she spun, she sang a strange song.

'First of eel, and second of hen,
And after that the fourth of wren.
Third of lean and first of meat,
Second of leg and third of feet.
Fifth of strong and second of pail,
Fourth of hammer and third of nail.
Sixth of button and third of coat,
First of me and second of boat.
When you've played this curious game,
You may perchance have found his name!'

The cat sang this over and over again, and the thrush listened hard. Soon she knew it by heart and at once flew off to the goblin's cottage. She put her head on one side and looked in at the window. Hoppetty was setting the table for the goblin and was talking to him.

'Is your name Twisty-Tail?'

'Ho, ho, ho! No, no, no!' roared the goblin.

'Well, is it Twisty-Nose?'

'Ho, ho, ho! No, no, no! And don't you be rude!' snapped the goblin.

'Well, is it Pointed-Ears?' asked poor Hoppetty.

'Ho, ho, ho! No, no, no! Give me some more jam cakes!' ordered the goblin.

The next day the thrush waited until the goblin had gone out, and then she began to sing sweetly.

Hoppetty knew that it was his own thrush singing, and he went to the window and listened – but what a peculiar song the bird was whistling! The thrush sang the cat's song over and over again – and suddenly Hoppetty guessed that it was trying to tell him how to find the goblin's name. He frowned and thought hard. Yes – he thought he could!

He fetched a pencil and a piece of paper and sat

down. The thrush flew to the windowsill and sang the song slowly. Hoppetty put down the words and then he began to work out the puzzle in great excitement.

'The first of eel – that's E. The second of hen – that's E too. The fourth of wren – that's N. The third of lean – A. The first of meat – M. Second of leg – another E. Third of feet – E again! Fifth of strong, that's N. Second of pail – A. Fourth of hammer – M. Third of nail – I. Sixth of button – N. Third of coat – A. First of me – M, and second of coat – O! Now what do all these letters spell?'

He wrote the letters out in a word, and looked at it – Eena-Meena-Mina-Mo!

'So that's the goblin's name!' cried the gnome in excitement. 'Oh, I would never, never have thought of that!'

The thrush flew off in a hurry, for she heard the goblin returning. He strode into his cottage and scowled when he saw the gnome sitting down writing instead of baking.

'What's all this?' he roared.

'Is your name Tabby-Cat?' asked the gnome with a grin.

'Ho, ho, ho! No, no, no!' cried the goblin. 'Get to your work.'

'Is it – is it – Wibbly-Wobbly?' asked the gnome, pretending to be frightened.

'Ho, ho, ho! No, no, no!' shouted the goblin in a rage. 'Where are my jam cakes?'

'Is it – can it be – Eena-Meena-Mina-Mo?' cried the gnome suddenly.

The goblin stared at Hoppetty and turned pale. 'How do you know that?' he asked in a frightened whisper. 'No one knows it! No one! Now you have found out my secret name! Oh! Oh! Go, you horrid creature! I am afraid of you! What will you find out next?'

He flung the door wide open, and Hoppetty ran out gladly, shouting:

'Eena, Meena, Mina, Mo,
Catch a goblin by his toe;
If he squeals, let him go,
Eena, Meena, Mina, Mo!'

He skipped all the way home – and there, sitting on his garden gate, was his friend the thrush. You can guess that Hoppetty gave her a fine meal of crumbs, and told her all about how angry and frightened the goblin was!

'I shall bake you a cake for yourself every time I have a baking day,' he promised. And he did – but, as you can guess, he never again made a jam cake or a chocolate finger!

Do Hurry Up, Dinah!

Do Hurry Up, Dinah!

ONCE UPON A time there was a little girl called Dinah. She was pretty and had nice manners, and she was kind and generous.

But oh, how slow she was!

You should just have seen her dressing in the morning. She took about five minutes finding a sock. Then she took another five minutes putting it on. Then she spent another five minutes taking it off because it was inside out. By the time she was dressed and downstairs everyone else had finished breakfast.

At breakfast time she was just as slow. You really would have laughed to see her eating her porridge.

First she sat staring at her plate. Then she put the sugar on very, very slowly and very, very carefully. Then she stared at the plate again. Then she put on her milk. She stirred the porridge slowly round and round and round, and then she began to eat it.

She took quite half an hour to eat it, so she was always late for school. And, dear me, when she did get to school what a time she took taking off her coat and hat. What a time she was getting out her pencil and rubber and book! By the time that Dinah was ready to begin her work, the lesson was finished.

She had two names. One was Slowcoach, which her mother called her, and the other was Tortoise, which her teacher called her.

'Dinah, you should have been born a tortoise!' her teacher used to say. 'You really should. You would have been quite happy as a slow old tortoise!'

'Well,' said Dinah, 'I wish I lived in Tortoise-Town, wherever it is! I hate people always saying "Do hurry up, Dinah, do hurry up, Dinah!" I'd like to live with tortoises. I'm sure they wouldn't keep hustling and bustling me like everyone else does.'

Now it so happened that the wind changed at the very moment that Dinah said this. You know that many strange things are said to happen when the wind changes, don't you? Well, sometimes a wish will come true at the exact change of the wind – and that's what happened to Dinah!

Her wish came true. She suddenly found that everything round her went quite dark, and she put out her hand to steady herself, for she felt giddy. She caught hold of something and held on to it tightly. The darkness gradually faded, and Dinah blinked her eyes. She looked round, expecting to see the schoolroom and all the boys and girls sitting down doing writing.

But she didn't see that. She saw something most strange and peculiar – so peculiar that the little girl blinked her eyes in astonishment.

She was in a little village street! The sun shone down

overhead, and around Dinah were funny little houses, with oval doors instead of oblong ones like ours.

She was holding on to something that was beginning to get very angry. 'Let go!' said a slow, deep voice. 'What's the matter? Let go, I say! Do you want to pull my shell off my back!'

Then, to Dinah's enormous surprise, she saw that she was holding tightly on to a tortoise as big as herself! He was standing on his hind legs, and he wore a blue coat, short yellow trousers, and a blue hat on his funny little wrinkled head.

Dinah stared at him in amazement. 'Who are you?' she asked.

'I'm Mr Crawl,' said the tortoise. 'Will you let go, please?'

Dinah let go. She was so surprised and puzzled at finding herself in a strange village all of a sudden with a tortoise walking by, that she could hardly say a word. But at last she spoke again.

'Where am I?' she asked.

'In Tortoise-Town,' said the tortoise. 'Dear me, I know you! You're the little girl that is called Tortoise at school, aren't you? You said you wanted to come here, didn't you – and here you are! Well, well – you'd better come home with me and my wife will look after you. Come along.'

'I want to go home,' said Dinah.

'You can't,' said Mr Crawl. 'Here you are and here you'll stay. No doubt about that. You should be pleased that your wish came true. Dear, dear, don't go so quickly. I can't possibly keep up with you!'

Dinah wasn't really going quickly. She always walked very slowly indeed – but the old tortoise shuffled along at the rate of about an inch a minute!

'Do hurry up!' said Dinah at last. 'I can't walk as slowly as this. I really can't.'

'My dear child, you were called Tortoise at school so you must be very, very slow,' said Mr Crawl. 'Now, here we are at last. There's Mrs Crawl at the door.'

It was all very astonishing to Dinah. She had passed

many tortoises in the road, some big, some small, all wearing clothes, and talking slowly to one another in their deep voices. Even the boy and girl tortoises walked very slowly indeed. Not one of them ran!

Mrs Crawl came slowly to meet Dinah and Mr Crawl. She did not look at all astonished to see Dinah.

'This little girl has come to live in Tortoise-Town,' said Mr Crawl. 'She needs somewhere to live, so I have brought her home.'

'Welcome!' said Mrs Crawl, and patted Dinah on the back with a clawed foot. 'I expect you are hungry, aren't you? We will soon have lunch! Can you smell it cooking?'

Dinah could and it smelt delicious. 'Sit down and I will get lunch,' said Mrs Crawl. Dinah sat down and watched Mrs Crawl get out a tablecloth.

It took her a long time to open the drawer. It took her even longer to shake out the cloth. It took her simply ages to lay it on the table! Then she began to lay the table with knives and forks and spoons. It took her over half an hour to do this and poor Dinah began to get more and more hungry.

'Let me put out the plates and glasses,' she said impatiently, and jumped up. She bustled round the table, putting the things here and there. Mrs Crawl looked at her crossly.

'Now, for goodness' sake don't go rushing about like that! It's bad for tortoises! It's no good getting out of breath and red in the face.'

'I'm not a tortoise,' said Dinah.

'Well, you soon will be when you have lived here a little while,' said Mr Crawl, who had spent all this time taking off one boot and putting on one slipper. 'You'll see – your hair will fall off and you'll be bald like us – and your neck will get wrinkled – and you'll grow a fine hard shell.'

Dinah stared at him in dismay. 'I don't want to grow into a tortoise!' she said.

Mr and Mrs Crawl gazed at Dinah in great annoyance. 'Rude little girl,' said Mrs Crawl. 'Go and wash your hands. Mr Crawl will go and wash his first and show you where to run the water.'

It took five minutes for Mr Crawl to walk to the washroom. It took him ten minutes to wash and dry himself, and by that time Mrs Crawl had actually got the lunch on the table. Dinah was so hungry that she washed her hands more quickly than she had ever washed them in her life before!

Oh, dear – what a long time Mr and Mrs Crawl took over their soup.

Dinah finished hers long before they were halfway through, and then had to sit and wait, feeling dreadfully hungry, while they finished. She fidgeted, and the two tortoises were cross.

'What an impatient child! Don't fidget so! Learn to be slower, for goodness' sake! You wanted to come and live with us, didn't you? Well, be patient and slow and careful.'

Lunch wasn't finished till four o'clock. *Almost teatime!* thought Dinah. *This is simply dreadful. I know*

now how horrid it must be for everyone when I am so slow at home or at school. They must feel as annoyed and impatient as I do now.

'I'll take you out for a walk when I'm ready,' said Mrs Crawl. 'There's a fair on in the marketplace, which perhaps you would like to see.'

'Oh, yes, I would!' cried Dinah. 'Oh, do hurry up, Mrs Crawl. I'm sure that by the time you've got your bonnet on, and your shawl, the fair will have gone!'

'Nobody ever says "Do hurry up!" in Tortoise-Town,' said Mrs Crawl, shocked. 'We all take our own time over everything. It's good to be slow. We never run, we never do anything quickly at all. You must learn to be much, much slower, dear child.'

It was six o'clock by the time that Mrs Crawl had got on her bonnet, changed her shoes and put on a nice shawl. Dinah thought that she had never in her life seen anyone so slow. Sometimes Mrs Crawl would stop what she was doing, and sit and stare into the air for quite a long time.

'Don't dream!' cried Dinah. 'Do hurry up!' And then she remembered how very, very often people had cried out the same thing to her, crossly and impatiently. *What a tiresome nuisance I must have been!* she thought. *Oh, dear – I didn't like hurrying up, but I hate even worse this having to be so slow!*

The fair was just closing down when they reached it. The roundabout was starting for the very last time. Dinah could have cried with disappointment. She got on to a horse, and the music began to play. The roundabout turned round very slowly indeed.

Dinah looked at all the creepy-crawly tortoises standing about, looking so solemn and slow, and she couldn't bear them.

'Oh, I wish I was back home!' she cried. 'I wish I was! I'd never be slow again, never!'

The roundabout horse that she was riding suddenly neighed loudly. Dinah almost fell off in surprise. It turned its head and looked at her. 'I'm a wishing-horse!' it said. 'Didn't you know? Be careful what you wish!'

The roundabout went faster. It went very fast indeed. Then it slowed down and stopped – and hey presto, what a surprise! Dinah was no longer in Tortoise-Town, but in a field at the bottom of her own garden! She knew it at once. She jumped off the horse and ran to the gate in her own garden wall. She looked back at the roundabout – and it slowly faded like smoke, and then it wasn't there any more.

Dinah tore up the garden path. She rushed down the passage to the kitchen. Her mother was there, and stared in amazement. She had never seen Dinah hurry herself before!

'What's happened to you?' she asked. 'You're really being quick for once.'

'I've been to Tortoise-Town!' said Dinah. 'And now I'm back again, hurrah! I'll never be a slowcoach or a tortoise again, never, never, never!'

She probably won't. Is there anyone you know that ought to go to Tortoise-Town? Not you, I hope!

The Goblin Hat

The Goblin Hat

THERE WAS ONCE a very mischievous goblin who had a magic hat. It was a very big one, with a wide, curly brim, and it was bright red except for its feather, which was blue.

It was a very magical hat. When the goblin put it on he couldn't be seen! It made him invisible at once.

But, of course, the hat could be seen, so it was a strange sight to see the hat bobbing along the street, its blue feather waving, and nobody underneath it! It made people feel very frightened indeed.

When the old Balloon Woman saw the hat coming along by itself, she gave a scream and ran away, leaving all her colourful balloons tied to the back of her chair. There weren't many of them left when at last she ventured back! The goblin had taken most of them, and was a mile away, with only his hat and the balloons to be seen!

And when he walked into Mr Buns' cake shop, the big hat bobbing on top of his invisible head and his footsteps going click-clack on the floor, Mr Buns fled to the room at the back of his shop at once.

There must be something wrong with my eyes! he thought. *And my ears too. I heard footsteps from feet I couldn't see, and saw a hat worn by somebody who wasn't there!*

Well, it didn't take long for the mischievous goblin to help himself to a big jam sandwich, a chocolate cake and a dozen jammy buns. Out he went, delighted, and everyone he met ran away in fright to see a big hat, a jam sandwich, a chocolate cake and a dozen buns bobbing along down the street. Even the butcher's fierce dog ran away, though he would dearly have liked to snap at the buns.

Now, Mr Plod the policeman was puzzled to hear these odd stories, but he soon got to the bottom of the mystery. 'It's Tiresome the goblin,' he said. 'He's got a big hat to wear that makes him invisible. Next time you see that hat, catch the invisible body below it, whip off the hat, and you'll see you've got Tiresome! Then bring him to me.'

Well, after that everyone waited for the hat to appear. But Tiresome the goblin heard about this, and he was frightened. He wasn't going to be caught! No, he knew what that would mean – scoldings and bread and water.

So what do you think he did? He went and caught Farmer Meadow's biggest billy goat, and he tied the magic hat to Billy's horns!

Well, of course, Billy vanished as soon as the hat was on his horns! He was there all right, but he couldn't be seen. Tiresome the goblin chuckled to himself and gave Billy a shove. 'Now, you go walking down the village street, looking as grand as can be in my hat – and don't you stand any nonsense from anyone!' he said.

So off went the billy goat, stepping proudly, not knowing that not a scrap of him could be seen except the hat. Down the village street he went and everyone yelled in excitement.

'Here's Tiresome the goblin! There's his hat, so he must be under it, though we can't see him. Catch him, catch him!'

'Leave this to me,' said Mr Stamp-About, who was always ready to show how clever he was. 'I'll manage him!'

He flung himself at the goat, thinking it was just a goblin he was getting hold of. Billy was most surprised. He put down his head and butted Mr Stamp-About so hard that he rolled into the gutter.

Mr Stamp-About was in a fine old temper when he got up. He rolled up his sleeves and rushed up to the hat, which was all he could see. The hat was bobbing about like anything, because the goat was prancing madly, ready to butt Mr Stamp-About again.

Mr Stamp-About made a grab at the hat, knowing

that if he could get it off, the person wearing it could easily be seen. But the hat was firmly tied to Billy's horns and wouldn't come off.

Poor Mr Stamp-About found himself butted and biffed, and although he tried to clutch at Billy here and there, Billy always got away.

'This goblin's hairy!' he cried. 'And my word, he's got a tail. Think of that! I felt it distinctly. I felt his beard too.'

Well, billy goats always wear beards and tails, so that wasn't surprising. Mr Stamp-About hadn't time to say any more because Billy butted him so hard that he flew into the air and landed in the middle of a case of Mr Apple's best tomatoes. After that Mr Stamp-About didn't want to have anything more to do with the hat.

Billy rushed at this person and that, butting and biffing happily. People went down like ninepins – and dear me, when Mr Plod the policeman came up, most surprised to see people tumbling about, Billy ran at him too!

Over he went, his helmet knocked down on his nose. 'What's all this?' he began. 'Oh – it's Tiresome the goblin, is it, behaving like this! That's his hat!'

Well, nobody could do anything with Billy the goat, and nobody could get the hat. People were beginning to get frightened, when somebody else came up the street. It was Tiresome the goblin, though nobody knew it! They had never seen him before, because he had always been invisible under his hat! He bowed politely.

'You seem to be in difficulties,' he said. 'I am Wise-One the magician. Can I help you?'

'Yes. Catch Tiresome the goblin – his hat's bobbing about over there!' yelled Mr Stamp-About. 'Look – I'll give you this bag of gold if you'll catch him!'

Tiresome took the bag of gold with a grin. He walked up to Billy, who knew him well, of course, and didn't attempt to butt him.

'Now, now,' said Tiresome, pretending to speak to a goblin, not a goat. 'You can't behave like this. You come along with me!'

The goat allowed himself to be led quietly up the street. When they were far enough away from everyone Tiresome unfastened the hat and took it off the goat's horns. Then Billy the goat followed him back to the busy marketplace.

'Thanks for the gold!' shouted Tiresome, waving the hat at everyone. 'I'm rich enough not to worry you any more! Goodbye!'

He clapped his hat on his head and became invisible at once. Everyone darted after him, yelling with rage – but Billy the goat met them once again, and they went flying. Oh dear, oh dear, what a terrible morning! They could see that magic hat bobbing away up the street and nobody dared to go after it.

'He's got my money!' wailed Mr Stamp-About. Mr Plod wrote a lot of things down in his notebook. 'One day we'll get that goblin,' he said. 'Yes, we will.

No doubt about that at all! Please notify me if anyone sees that HAT.'

Well, it's not very likely that we'll see it but you never know. In case you do, here's Mr Plod's telephone number – PLO 24681357000!

Acknowledgements

All efforts have been made to seek necessary permissions. The stories in this publication first appeared in the following publications:

'The Lost Motorcar' first appeared in *Enid Blyton's Sunny Stories,* No. 281, 1942.

'Loppy and the Witch' first appeared in *The Teachers World*, No. 1456, 1931.

'Mary, Mary, Quite Contrary' first appeared in *The Teachers World*, No. 1021, 1924.

'The Spick-and-Span Stone' first appeared in *The Teacher's Treasury (Vol.1)* published by The Home Library Book Company, 1926.

'He Couldn't Do It!' first appeared in *The Big Enid Blyton Book* published by Paul Hamlyn, 1961.

'Betsy's Fairy Doll' first appeared in *Sunny Stories for Little Folks,* No. 178, 1933.

'The King's Treasure' first appeared in *The Teachers World*, No. 1610, 1934.

'The Dirty Old Hat' first appeared in *Enid Blyton's Sunny Stories*, No. 377, 1946.

'The Pinned-On Tail' first appeared in *Enid Blyton's Sunny Stories*, No. 16, 1937.

'Snippitty's Shears' first appeared in *Sunny Stories for Little Folks*, No. 138, 1932.

'The Good Luck Morning' first appeared in *Enid Blyton's Sunny Stories*, No. 412, 1947.

'Floppety Castle' first appeared in *Fairyland Tales*, No. 40, 1922.

'The Wizard's Umbrella' first appeared in *Sunny Stories for Little Folks*, No. 202, 1934.

'My Goodness, What a Joke!' first appeared as 'My Goodness – What a Joke' in *The Evening Standard*, No. 38,897, 1949.

'The Fairy and the Policeman' first appeared in *Sunny Stories for Little Folks*, No. 147, 1932.

'Who Came Creeping in the Door?' first appeared in *Enid Blyton's Sunny Stories*, No. 398, 1947.

'Roundy and the Keys' first appeared in *The Teachers World*, No. 1186, 1926.

'Mr Pink-Whistle is a Conjurer!' first appeared in *Enid Blyton's Magazine*, No. 17 Vol. 6, 1958.

'Tick-Tock's Tea Party' first appeared in *Sunny Stories for Little Folks*, No. 201, 1934.

'The Fly-Away Cottage' first appeared in *Sunny Stories for Little Folks*, No. 196, 1934.

'Winkle Makes a Mistake' first appeared in *Sunny Stories for Little Folks*, No. 224, 1935.

'The Little Clockwinder' first appeared in *The Teachers World*, No. 1622, 1934.

'Tell Me My Name!' first appeared in *Enid Blyton's Sunny Stories*, No. 8, 1937.

'Do Hurry Up, Dinah!' first appeared in *Enid Blyton's Sunny Stories*, No. 314, 1943.

'The Goblin Hat' first appeared in *Enid Blyton's Sunny Stories*, No. 450, 1949.

Also look out for:
Enid Blyton
25 stories
STORIES OF
SPELLS
AND
ENCHANTMENTS
A dazzling collection of magical tales by the world's best-loved storyteller.

There's magic and wonder brewing in this bumper collection by the world's best-loved storyteller.

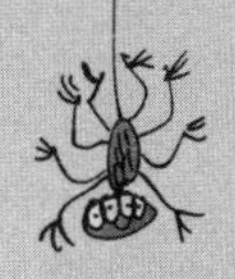

Also look out for:

A magical collection of short stories from the world's best-loved storyteller!

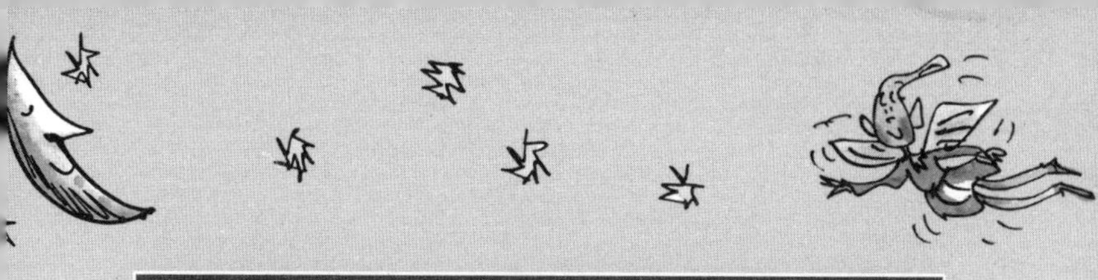

Find magic and mischief in these short stories by the world's best-loved storyteller.